Kind words

I read *Daddio!* in almost one sitting. I couldn't stop reading it: I was captivated, utterly swept up in it. I cannot imagine the pain that the author has lived to have been able to write it, but he has transmuted life's base matter into literary gold. It's just brilliant. I'm so happy to have read it. It glitters with intelligence, and that fierce need to tell the truth.
Jay Griffiths, author of *Wild* and *Why Rebel*

Lovely, mighty, and very funny.
Paul Ewen, author of *Francis Plug: How to be a Public Author*

Daddio! is a lot of fun—imagine going for a three-hour car ride with your deadbeat dad, an unopened can of worms, and a bunch of fascists and angels. I was instantly immersed in the story; the language is playful and the dialogues made me laugh. Lockwood drew me close to his sensitive protagonist, who notices every detail, every shift in mood and tone, and all the hidden messages that his family members don't even notice they're sending out. I found it relatable and moving how the protagonist goes back and forth between a hopeful loving of his family and the planet, and a hopeless grappling with the bleak state both are really in. The novel gradually introduces the possibility of shifting realities so the experience of both trying to heal your family and heal the climate crisis become entwined, monstrous and symbolic. And yet the ending is gentle, a soft closing of a door (or the lid of a can).
Bette Adriaanse, author of *What's Mine*

Also by HardArt . Metalabel

https://hardart.metalabel.com/

Drawn Without Looking
(Ian Bruce and friends)

The Fête of Britain
(collaborative)

The Work WE Need to To
(collaborative)

Also by Alex Lockwood

The Pig in Thin Air

The Chernobyl Privileges

DADDIO!

The HardArt Collective

HARDART . METALABEL

HardArt . Metalabel
First published in Great Britain by HardArt . Metalabel 2025
Copyright (c) Alex Lockwood 2025

The moral right of Alex Lockwood to be identified as the author of this work has been asserted in accordance with the dodgy capitalist practices of the Copyright, Designs & Patents Act 1988.

Although ...while some rights are reserved (but which ones? do I even know?!) reproduction, copy or transmission of this publication may be made with written enthusiasm and *is encouraged*; please get in touch. We are living in sight of the collapse of our ecological, social, economic and political systems where statements made under laws such as the Copyright Act 1988 will soon mean zip, zilch, nada. We are psychically preparing ourselves and each other to live in collaboration and kindness, and that will entail forms of sharing that may feel radical right now (such as giving away your intellectual property, or indeed your physical property) but that in a short time will be necessary: a matter of life and death. In that spirit, we bid you to quote, borrow, copy, remix, and share the material in this book and the accompanying release (supported via Metalabel). The collective of Hard Art bids you to begin imagining how life will be when we collaborate together *again* under the Radical Sharing Act 2036.

Always remember: humanity is love. Give it for free!

A CIP record for this title is available from the British Library until it is under water.

ISBN: 978-1-906180-25-6 (paperback)

Cover image drawn by Jeremy Deller. Thank you.
Illustration (opposite) by Bette Adriaanse. Thank you.
Cover by Clive Russell, in Guppy Blue (made it up). Thank you.

Typeset in Dante Medium 11pt by Absurd Intelligence.
Printed and bound by Taylor Brothers, Bristol, BS4 4EU.

for

Phil (1948-2022)
Misha (2008-2023)
& Chris (1974-2024)

"Now, surely, the great final change must be approaching, come now and take me to be for ever with Thee in Thy Paradise! I am ready to come. My heart is purged from sin, there is nothing now that keeps me rooted to this wicked world. Oh, come now, and take me before I have known the temptations of life, before I have to go to London and all the dreadful things that happen there!"

— **Edmund Gosse,** *Father and Son*

Foreword

This book is abominably funny.

A man is on his way to his sister's funeral, taking his elderly and evil-tempered father (he of the necrotizing feet.)

They never arrive, as the story of their family's horribly authentic dysfunctionality is a can o' worms the protagonist must not open and yet is compelled to. They also never arrive as shards of the known future slash through the man's experience, heat beyond endurance and seasickening floods.

Gnarled memories of the twisted entaglement that is the common torture of the nuclear family are translated with morbid and glittering brilliance. Scenes of domestic life are strewn across the book like smashed crockery but then gathered by the narrator into a profound mending where nothing may be fixable but everything is at least sayable. The book blazes with the unflinching need to speak honestly.

Set partly in the near-future, the book is a portrayal of the polycrisis we are in, a crisis of health, of democracy, of education, of extinctions, of climate, and a crisis of truth. In the personal context, there is the inevitable crisis of ordinary people whose pain is imposed by ideologies of power.

It is a tale told in the gut language of gut intelligence where soured relationships reach the peak-curdle moment of human pain recognizable across all the cell walls, telling the reader: you are not alone.

You may read this book to feel understood.

You may read it for its gothic gallows humour.

You may read it for its sheer brilliance of notation, in the known unknowns of the acknowledged human heart.

You may read it for its revelation of visceral crisis already being felt by so many people across the world: where the air is an oven; where the waters may drown you; where drought or flood leaves the fertile earth ineluctably undone, famine in the wings and wildfire out of control.

You may read it because the element of human imagination—the alchemical quintessence—is more precious than lithium, iridium, palladium or platinum. But please read it.

This book is being presented through **HardArt**, a hive-mind of political artists, directors, musicians, designers, producers, makers, writers with some salt-of-the, for rootedness. **HardArt** is committed to an unflinching stance: *Tell the truth: we're fucked if we don't make radical changes at radical speed.* What passes for democracy has been nabbed by the wealthy, and we the citizens want it back. It gives steady support to Citizens' Assemblies as the golden sword that can cut through the ugly knots of a political world crazed with psychopaths, clowns and junk-tanks. **HardArt** is a movement of the heart that holds to love, respect and mycelial intelligence. **HardArt** is a movement in service to all that matters: fairness, the furry world of the animals, kindness, hospitality of the heart, human dignity, football and—beyond and before and between and behind everything—Life.

Jay Griffiths is a HardArtist and an award-winning author of *Wild: An Elemental Journey*, *Why Rebel* and *how animals heal us*. She is also a wild skater when the Welsh lakes freeze, if they ever will again.

Any likeness to persons living or dead is mathematically, somewhere across the universal field, bang on. But on this litigious planet, the collaborative asserts that this is a work of fiction, and any similarities with those living, dead, or somewhere caught in between, are mostly (mostly!) made up.

GETTING HIM TO THE FUNERAL presented a number of challenges.

One: His feet. He didn't really have them. What was left was rebandaged on Monday afternoons by a nurse at the health centre. It was the smoking, mainly, that did for them. He claimed there was some remarkable virus to blame, something he'd picked up while a child in Africa when his father, my grandfather, was posted there with the Coldstream Guards in the nineteen fifties. By the end of that decade my father had become the oldest of six children, and six, apparently, was one too many to cope with while fighting the Cold War and the hot jungle, six the number at which the domestic scales tipped. So while the rest of his family unit—his father, mother and five siblings—marched forward on their worldwide army tour, my father was jettisoned in Glasgow to live with Granny, a great-grandparent I never met. He became acquainted with Govan and the Gorbals and no doubt many more granite façades than were to be found in Kenya or Yemen. It had sat dormant inside him for a good sixty years, he'd told me once, this suspicious bugaboo (the virus, but also, I assumed, the jettisoning). Yet when I googled 'African virus that eats your feet', amidst the gory but fascinating images of *necrotizing fasciitis* there wasn't anything that matched his condition. Except Buerger's Disease, where blood vessels become inflamed, swollen and blocked with blood clots, first appearing as wasting in the extremities. And to be fair it *was* prevalent in Africa, but only in that *virtually everyone diagnosed with Buerger's Disease smokes cigarettes or uses other forms of the drug such as chewing tobacco.* Was he, pre-jettison, smoking on the streets of Nairobi at eight? Quite possibly. And for Buerger's Disease (*thromboangiitis obliterans*) quitting tobacco was the only cure.

He never had. He still smoked ten a day. But he used crutches not a wheelchair and his mobility on the crutches, for having Buergered-up feet, wasn't the worst. It gave me some hope for our manoeuvres: I would drive him to the funeral parlour, then the crematorium, and back again from the wake, during which he could sit or plod as he needed without me on hand to wheel him about. But here was the problem: the funeral was on a Monday, so no trip to the nurse, so his bandages would be a week old; encrusted, odorous, and causing him pain. Not really what you want at a funeral, for the living or the dead.

'Can you get another appointment?' I asked on my prior visit. 'Later in the week?'

He shook his head, his yellow moustache waggling in the sour air of the bedsit.

'Twice in a week? Fucking hard enough to get the one I have.'

Two: an old person's fear of upsetting the delicate routine.

'Couldn't you arrange the funeral for a fucking Friday?'

Three: expletive stubbornness that somehow makes everything your (my) fault.

Four: (returning to the African virus) a weakness for making things up. He shared that trait with my sister. Both fashioned stories which they told to others and then came to believe themselves. I knew why I di—*had* done it. Tried not to any more. He did still, but then at seventy-six there was no stopping him now (his moustache reminded me of Freddie Mercury). My sister, she was never gonna give them up either, these comforting deceptions. Case in point: at her wedding a handful of months earlier, Tracy, a friend and manager at high street store Iceland, who'd tried to interest me in having an affair while her husband of nineteen years sat not two tables away, shook her head as she told me how amazing it was,

To see her (my sister) *happy after all she's been through.*

Been through? (I asked) *Like what?*

Like your dad breaking every bone in her body.

I'd had a few drinks by then. The evening 'do' was in a small dirty marquee out back of The White Swan, dodgy Dave's disco keeping the kids entertained, and there wasn't a single sandwich from the buffet suitable for my ethical tastes. So I gave Tracy what for. *That's bullshit. It never happened.* Tracy, bless her, didn't know where to look. At her feet, maybe. Which were still intact when she walked off a few minutes later with the begrudged hubby.

Five, toughest: the relationship between my sister and father ended, for all intents and purposes (much intent, no purpose) thirty-five years ago. They'd had, to the best of my knowledge, zero contact since. And it wasn't going to start up anytime soon, bearing in mind I was here to get *him* to *her* funeral.

'The door was open,' he grumbled, stubbing out a cigarette in the sink. He sat in a highchair for adults, for the rickety. A sudden fleeting memory of my mother perched similarly to do the washing up, wilting like a sick geranium in the pot. 'Why'd you knock?'

'Because you knock when you go into someone else's—' it wasn't a house, not even a flat. A ground floor supported-living bedsit with the thermostat set to melting icecaps. A few plodcrutch steps from single bed to armchair to kitchen table to three ring hob, everything a grim filmy beige. I didn't finish my sentence. I looked around. 'Are you ready?'

He most obviously wasn't. He was topless while smoking at the sink. His belly—my belly, too, I was coming to realise, as I aged—paunched over his jeans. His jeans were stained with soup and whisky. His whisky—his supported-living supervisor toured Scottish distilleries and brought back póitinous contraband—on the side table by his armchair. The crutches propped against the fridge; the fridge's bottom draw filled with mini chocolate bars. He performed his laugh then, the one to express incredulity at my stupid statement, inane question, or generally disappointing deed. It was a laugh that had come to be an expression of his astonishment at my very existence, haloed as I had become in the patio doorway of his bedsit, somewhere he'd never expected to see me, his son, after all the time that had passed.

Six: could I spend an entire day with my father?

At the funeral I could hand him onto my uncle, on my mother's side, who'd always liked my dad, and had a greater tolerance for people than I could muster. As the brother of the deceased, I would have licence to wander, even dip out of the wake to go *feel my feelings*. As the estranged father of the deceased he would too; but having to mostly sit because of his feet, he'd be reliant on those who showed pity with him to parlay. Maybe Tracy. See how long they lasted.

Seven: he was nasty without a drink and bitter with.

Eight: he smelled bad. He and the bedsit had merged olfaction. But then, if this was his life—few visitors, a single malt for the week, reruns of black & white Ealing noirs, pondering the state of the nation as brought to him by GBNews, and life's intent now given over to the *Biggest Book of Sudoku and Word Puzzles*—I suppose you forgot not to offend the senses.

Nine (related to *Five*): I'd been told not to bring him by my sister's widower, Gavin. *Don't bring that bastard.* I did know my sister *she wouldn't want him here* wouldn't want him there. She'd called our mum's third husband *dad*. I'm glad she found her replacement in the dad aisle. When I'd found our father (sticking with the original!) after his fifteen-year disappearing act, she didn't want to know *couldn't face it* my aunt relayed the message to me, my sister had not processed the past *inner work capable of facing him* (said my therapist) as *you have* (same therapist) I had (only just).

Ten: don't open the can. Cans of familial worms should not be opened.

Not above ten. Ten was enough.

Dad picked up his crutches and bumbled off, I presumed, to a hallway wardrobe. I'd come in through the French patio doors (bit of a posh name for them, here in this egress of south London), which opened straight into the bedsit. I didn't know if there were more rooms back there—more than a bathroom, anyway—as on my visits I'd only got as far as the kitchen table. I sat and waited. Among the mess of shopping lists and tea mugs and ashtrays there was a copy of my book under the crosswords and TV magazines. I'd sent it to him as an easier way to explain what I did: show not tell. Fifteen years had passed quickly for both of us, although I'd done a few things in that time worth sharing, perhaps. I'd visited half a dozen times since his unsought reappearance (unsought by him), plucking daddio from the obscurities as a semi-missing person with the help of a private investigator and credit ratings. They weren't awful to begin with, those visits. But, if I forget to mention them, ask:

about the two cream doughnuts,
about what he said about my book,
what he said about his family, the jettisoners: mother father sisters and brothers.

He'd not seen *my* sister in those lost fifteen years, in fact longer, after she'd discarded him before he disappeared. But, living or dead, she *was* his daughter. When I'd first found him, he'd asked after her. I'd told him she was getting married. Was he invited? Tangible pain on his face when I said she'd not wanted to see him.

(But ask about that too. What he said when I told him she didn't want to see him.)

He came back from the hallway, *hallelujah!*, dressed now at least, but wearing a top you'd expect to see at the World Darts Championships: shiny black front panels sporting a kind of dragon design in silvery sheen, wide flat lapels showing too much chest hair. I wouldn't have been surprised if he'd put his darts in the breast pocket just in case The White Swan... indeed. Same venue, same small dirty marquee, wedding and funeral 'dos' six months apart. I hardened my stare to stop the eyes from leaking; stared at his shirt; no, at least he'd not packed the darts. He'd not changed his jeans either, though. I stymied the tears by trying hard not to look at his bandaged half-feet. But I was in no doubt of at least one thing: this look of his was not going to slip in unnoticed at the back of the service, was it?

'Do you need a coat?'

'Nah, nahimbaemae,' he replied, his signature two-tone mumble that I had come to comprehend as a blanket negation; the first *nah* a high-pitched refusal, the second *nah* lower, trailing away into denegations I could neither hear nor did he ever finish anyway. Didn't need to, when tone was all. So tonal! Did he (we) have

Chinese ancestry?

'Okay then, let's go.'

I pushed aside the thick net curtains and stepped outside. On the patio next door three people sat around a black metal garden table having a breakfast smoke. They didn't stop chatting. I waited for dad. I couldn't see back through the netting, but hoped he wasn't having a breakfast whisky. Or hoped he was. There was a sweet spot where the drink made him less misericious than sober, before it pushed him into full blown *open the can* mode. (Case in point: my 18th birthday. *If you think I'm a cunt,* he garbled as he held himself up on the kitchen doorframe *call me a cunt.*)

(I didn't call him a cunt. I thought it. But I was the sober one. On my 18th birthday!)

(Miserably vicious.)

To be fair, I would've said yes to a breakfast whisky right then if he'd offered.

'Alright there!' one of the neighbours called over, fag between third and fourth fingers, a dexterity I found more fascinating than it warranted (but, no!, if the fag were chopsticks or a silver coin this digital-magician would be on a national telly talent contest).

'Ah alright,' my dad replied, studying the concrete where his crutches landed like pikes. He pointed at me. 'My son,' as if the others had demanded an explanation.

'Hello *son*,' the three neighbours chorused with waves. I waved back, trying but failing to see how the other two held their cigarettes. Chatter ensued. I nipped to the car and opened the back door for him to throw in his crutches.

'Nah, nahimbaemae,' which I interpreted, as it came with another wave of the crutch, that I didn't nee—'to fucking cosset me.'

Translation in real time! Eat your heart out, owly android app.

Crutches in the footwell, he contrived his way into the passenger seat and the smell of his clothing overwhelmed me. I made a show of wiping away the inner condensation then opened my window and put on the aircon. I put the phone in its cradle and typed in the funeral parlour where we would meet the others as destination. He shook his head. Christ, a digital map! What a failure of my navigation skills! A memory twisted through my cortex: of driving my dad for the first time after I'd bought my inaugural car, a boy racer, blue Triumph Dolomite Sprint with a dodgy gearbox, purchased, to be fair, with the £1,000 he gave me for my 18th (before the cuntydoorframe episode), then him asking *why the fuck you've wasted the money on a jalopy?* I don't remember answering. I didn't ask why he hadn't helped me buy a car, other than bung me the money and wait for me to make disappointing investments with it. His gravestone was to read *Gave You Enough Rope...* (if I had anything to do with it).

Ten ten ten ten ten. Don't open the can.

I took a surreptitious deep breath through the window-side of my mouth.

'Why aren't you going left?'

'It says *Similar ETA*,' I pointed at the map.

'How long we got? Four hours?'

I nodded. Actually we had five, but I didn't want to be late. And if we did get there early it was easy enough to go for two—but no more than two!—drinks.

'Go left then.'

'We can go either.'

'Nah,' high pitched, shake of the head, shoulder shrug, so high pitched!, 'nahimbaemae.'

The translate function for such noises does not sit in the ear, by the way, but in the gut.

Then we were off.

I was hyperconscious of his being next to me—a feeling not dissimilar to a bad first date, all expectation and awkwardness and wanting it to be over. We drove north because Google said so and Google could take the heat from my dad's dribbling wrath. He professed to not understand how smartphones worked. That was established at our first meeting: he'd used it as an excuse for not searching for me online in his fifteen years hiding out in the wildernesses of SE25. Mind, there was no wrath in those first few miles of the drive, at maps or me, only the wet cavernous alarm of his breathing. He was infirmly unfit, despite forcing himself to work out most days up and down the sheltered housing stairs. He had COPD (Chronic Obstructive Pulmonary Disease; plenty of dark humour in the hospitals with that: *'Oh, he COP'D it in the night!'*) so it took a while for his lungs to return to rest after exertions, such as getting in a car. No suspicion about this particular ailment; it was flagrant and unsettling. His lungs rattled, his moustache twitched in tune. Had he gotten used to the frightening sounds emanating from his ribcage? I didn't ask, not only because he was incapable of answering. I drove on, into central London so we could meet the North Circular, then east to connect with the A12 then the A14, heading to the coast. Only three hours in the car, nothing to fear!

*

I should probably get to my sister. Explain why she never spoke to him again, how (or because) the *every bone in her body* was made up. How she died. Or I could flash back to the moment I registered daddio as a missing person, only to give up looking after a year and to let it slide for the next fifteen. (I *did* look, at least; charities were involved, although they were more concerned with children on the streets, not sour drunks in bedsits.) I could leap to his year unconscious in the hospital. Or why, after a decade and a half, I renewed my pursuit with the hire of a private investigator. I expected dad to be dead, but—just my luck!—he was alive, nary a mile from where we grew up. I could begin six hundred and nine other places.

But let's get to the two cream doughnuts.

The PI gave me an address from the credit records but no phone number. I could've written and given him warning, but what would be the point? I surprised him. He said he didn't recognise me at first (I question that) and we didn't speak much. There were lots of long looks, shakings of the head. After forty-five minutes I departed to let my apparition settle into a solid. I told him I'd be back in a few weeks to take him for a (nasty-without-*sweet-spot*-call-me-a-cunt) drink. I then went and sat in my car, and tears burst out of me—which is different, it's worth noting, from crying.

The night before that return visit, I had a dream. I was buying lunch from an airport Boots concession, but they'd run out of sandwiches. The only food left in the droning Frigidaire was an out-of-date pack of avocado sushi. Just then an old university friend Thalia (named for the Greek goddess of comedy) passed by, saying *you don't want that vegan shit, you want these two cream doughnuts* which she held out in a tatty presentation box. I refused, I didn't eat dairy, baby calves n' all, but she insisted. *Go on, have these TWO CREAM DOUGHNUTS*.

So. I visit my dad and take him out for a drink. The first conversation for fifteen years, the first drink we'd had in over twenty. We're sitting having a pint of Guinness in the nearby Harvester pub, where, as it happened, I used to come with friends thirty years earlier on a Thursday night, after police cadets (like sea cadets or scouts, but with truncheons and riot training). We'd drive to the pub in the drugs van: not an official police wagon, but a VW Camper owned by one of the cadets, which we would steer into the middle of nowhere—east London in those days—to take drugs, mainly speed (the rest of the crew became Met Police officers, it won't surprise you). Anyway, my dad and I are sitting having a pint of Guinness and he's telling me about his life. He *also* has a Thursday routine, this one still active, where a taxi picks him up and he heads to the Sainsbury's behind Crystal Palace football ground and makes the most of the early morning *doddery cunt hour* for people shielding from Covid or who are generally old/and disabled. The taxi waits for him while he does his shopping. Now, the reason I couldn't find him when he went missing fifteen years prior was that, for a year, daddio was in hospital in a coma after his body collapsed, indeed *he* collapsed, after a bender, and it just so happened with no ID on his person, having either lost it or had it robbed in his paralyticism. His time in a coma included a number of heart attacks. He'd lived hard enough, been through enough, to die then. But no. He was discharged from hospital after a year following rehabilitation and losing most of his feet. So this discharging consultant tells daddio *you shouldn't smoke or drink again, but that'll probably kill you faster than keeping the crutches* (he meant the smoking and drinking crutches, not the walking crutches), which made sense to my dad because, according to him, *only time I ever caught a fucking cold was when I gave up the fags*. Understandable, him having smoked and drank since he was twelve (possibly an African eight; but, anyway, what else was a working-class Glaswegian boy to do? See a therapist? Thrust oneself into *inner work*?). So, this consultant says to my dad *cut it all down, but make sure you don't go into withdrawal; in fact, spoil yourself a bit* (which you could argue he'd done for all his life, and many others lives too). My dad, never one, as far as I remembered, for treats, now gets to Sainsbury's before the *doddery old fuckers,* the taxi waiting outside, him stalking inside, and the first thing he does *because if I don't they're gone* and that *upsets my routine* is head to the bakery and *treat myself to*

TWO CREAM DOUGHNUTS.

Goddess of comedy!

I'm sipping my Guinness as he tells me, hiding my smirk. To be honest, I'm not surprised. Aware of a little quantum field theory (although no doubt mangling the physics) it is supposed that time is not an arrow but a field on which all things have already happened, including this moment now. For superluminal beings travelling faster than light (The Flash in the DC Comics Multiverse comes to mind) there is one dimension of space but *three* of time: time past, time present, and time future. Each dimension is navigable to superluminal beings, as easily as our left and right, up and down. Of course I'm no superluminary being (yet). But there's no other way I could have known about his two cream doughnuts routine, is there? Not across the *normal* field of things. Growing up I never saw him eat sweet treats. I don't eat cream doughnuts myself. *And we'd not talked for twenty years.* So, how *else* could I have known in advance of his cream doughnut habit, unless my dream *wasn't* simply a dream but a thought-is-faster-than-light slip across the universal field? Still sipping on my Guinness, I accepted this touch of psyche*deli* divination as a reward. But for what? For my healing efforts? The *inner work* that had prepared me to search for my dad after fifteen years? Sure, why not! The healing had, clearly, attuned me to pass through an unconscious gateway in which I'd hooked up to an alternative power assembly, a superposition between two beings (I–dad) bound across time, cream-father like doughnut-son, universally connected despite decades of earthly separation. Yet what stronger fabric could there be to weave the universal tent than that of love. Or genes. Or the combination of the two: *blood*.

Well, perhaps.

Either way, I *had* already known what my father had just then told me over that pint. About the doughnuts. But not *only* about the doughnuts. Rather, this was a sign, was it not, about the *deeper why* of sitting there with him after two decades; why I'd finally healed enough to search for him; why I was, right at that moment, chauffeuring my father to his daughter's interment. I felt it was even deeper than that: this was not only a message for me, but a transcendent sign for everyone: what we are *all* here for. That is, if I can get to the point (and back to the driving), my father's two cream doughnuts taught me this: we may not know the universe's plan for us (there may not *be* a plan as such) but what there *is,* is the possibility of a superluminal connection across the multiversal field which makes it as clear as day to anyone paying attention that it's all made out of—yes, love! Genes! Blood! So! Mark the doughnuts. Be assured that right here right now is where we are *meant* to be. And so that means *who* we are with, too. Right? I suppose the Ayahuasca retreats to Peru influenced this doughnut episode. Had those psychedelic trips unlocked a precognitive dreaming? No reason why not. Under the sway of the shaman there is no linear time; in fact no time at all.

The retreats had been a grand gesture to mark the end (ha!) of a cycle of healing. 'End (ha!)' because:

one, it never ends of course (Exhibit A: *the can*); and

two, because you can't simply *choose* to have trauma be done with; even if the shaman says you are cleansed, the scars don't disappear.

So I counselled myself: the doughnuts were sign enough for me to know that I should be here with my father. No further can opening. Not by me. No deep diving into the murky past with the man who came out of his coma and didn't bother to contact his family to tell them he was alive. No stirring shit with the shitty stick for he who had droppethed off the earth (half a mile from where we saw him last). *Nah, nahimbaemae* to you, too, daddio.

But, even if you're adamant about not opening the can, the can will be opened when it is good and ready, by forces beyond your control. And lo, the great spiritual consciousness of the universe is awoken! And she is interested not in petty human attempts to evade awkward conversations, but in epiphanic destiny. I was umbilically tied to my dad in the universal field through my effort of healing; the universal consciousness was wont to manifest such connection by occasionally poking one in the ribs about it. *Think you'll get away with unopening the can, matey?* says she. *On a three-hour drive to a funeral?! You think you'll avoid the* buried *stuff? Think again.*

But no, no, no. No can. I was putting my foot down (metaphorically and, as it happened, literally). One day, that was all. My job was just this: get him to the funeral (and back).

*

We drove past the Beulah Spa Harvester, scene of Thursday night police cadet underage speeding *and* now of the superluminary doughnut-shaped revelation. Then past the girls' school where I once got my head stuck in a number 19 bus's window shouting '*Oi, what's your name?*' at one of the girls (an out-of-character dare). Then we approached my old school and the Thompson Engineering factory opposite. Dad got me my first job there, sweeping the office and shop floors after school for the bossman, Peter, an Indian who smoked eighty a day and was dead by forty-nine from lung cancer (*COP'D it!*). My dad was a manager for the company but in their second factory over in Deptford. He seethed about why Peter got the red Lancia for a company car and my dad only the Vauxhall

Vectra (I guessed, but didn't volunteer out loud, because *drink-drive record*, daddio?). This factory had since closed and become a vintage car showroom. I looked over as we passed, expecting him to say something about the time I let him down when I failed to press Peter for a pay rise, or one of the other disappointing episodes in my early working life. But he was still reconstituting his lungs.

My old school, on the other side of the road, had been Catholic, its grand yellow façade with the golden gargoyles once the home of George VI's bookmaker. My dad, an atheist (protestant at best, when at the Glasgow Rangers pubs) was not pleased, especially when discovering it was run by monks. But then I guess when you run off with another woman and leave your wife with two kids under four and your marriage is decreed *nisi*, you get less say in such matters.

'Do you remem—' I began. Oh. What was I *doing?!* The can, the can!

'Wha?' he asked, turning not towards me but away. As if he *did* remem—. But with all my concentration on *his* rattling, I hadn't noticed *my* nerves clanking. Too late now!

'Do you remember when I showed you my G.C.S.E. results?'

He looked dead forward, a laugh and then a deep, phlegmy cough caught in a fleshy underbite, the jowly flop of a man with few teeth, and he swallowed whatever he'd coughed up. I winced. He then rocked his head as if either:

a) he *did* remem(ber) what he'd said when I showed him my G.C.S.E. results, and was now shaking the memory out of his ear so as not to have to admit to it; *or*,

b) this rocking his head was a tic when put on the spot, a nerve-ending response to not knowing how to deal with the lifelong pain of fucking up one's loves so badly. Either was terrible, right? Either was the shit buried deep under the worms that I didn't want to go digging for. What was I, some sort of trauma angler? A Swiss Army Knife of distress? No! I was neither so emotionally incisive nor so deeply murked. I checked the dashboard: twenty-three minutes into the journey, Christ!

'Just because—my school,' I blathered, the building receding in the mirrors.

'I can'ae fucking remember last week, my memory's gone,' he said. He was shaking, perhaps from lung pressure, perhaps at a question that had obviously (*obviously!*) been the wrong thing to ask: couldn't *I* remember he couldn't remember things?! But he brightened, in a way I'd come to recognise. He had suddenly recalled something, a pre-planned question, something he'd jotted down in the margins of a word puzzle to come back to, a trick to keep it in the medium-term grey matter where things once in a while stuck. He'd try to make it spontaneous, and almost nothing about his still being alive made me sadder than this slightly desperate need to prepare in advance what to ask me. Because it was not about his memory, not completely. In his lonelier moments in his filmy beige bedsit he felt a want to reach out to me with love and curiosity, and had made a plan for how to do it. But when it came to the execution, he had none of the facility to make it work. The question came out forced, and it crumpled under the weight of what we carried between us. (Of course this showed up the lack of *my* relational skills too. I didn't handle the stilted offering well.)

'That's what I was going to ask you...'

'Okay, go on...'

He bouted with another cough as I turned left at the lights, leaving behind my old school and its memories. We headed down the hill into Streatham, passing the tree under which I had my first kiss (with Kris with a K, in a button-up orange paisley jumper. Me, not her).

'What's wrong with eggs?'

'What's wrong with *eggs*?'

'Why don't vegans eat 'em?'

(Was it a good kiss? Maybe not; the next week Kris with a K was with Jayson with a Y.)

Then *I* was seething: at Google. This route *was* a trip down memory lane. But that gave rise to a sadness of not being able to *share* those memories, because I was with the person who made those memories so clouded, tainted, painful. Why *this* route, Google? Was I being led to be kind to him so he could be kind to me? Before *he* died? Nah, nahimbaemae.

I puffed out my cheeks and blew air. Okay, then. Eggs.

'It's a cruel industry. You hear a lot about free range but even they don't get—and most aren't free range anyway. Bird flu, they're all indoor—. Did you know we've pushed their bodies so much to lay more—like 300 a year—so most hens die from reproductive issues. Like ovarian canc—'

'Well fuck me,' he said, breaking into one of his laughs at the cruel irony of animal life.

'What?'—*the fuck,* I wondered, was so funny about the cancerous sufferings of chickens?

He squealed then like a mouse. It took a while to calm.

'That's where I met your mother.'

What?

'Where?'

We were stopped at a pedestrian crossing on Streatham High Street outside a now closed nightclub, at which he was pointing. When I was fifteen, a group of us older-looking boys from school would come on a Tuesday night to *this very nightclub*, then called The Ritzy, for a few pints of lager and lime, a bit of dancing, and some talking *about* rather than *with* any of the girls whose faces dazzled us in the purple and green lights of disco. The Ritzy had changed management and names to become Caesar's before it closed, and the building still had charioteering horses leaping from the façade above double doors, now shuttered and littered with the remnants of the rough sleepers who made it their temporary stables.

'You met mum in *there*?'

Shivery, the thought I'd danced on the same dancefloor—and never knew!

'It was the Cat's Whiskers then.' Green light, drive on. Horses rearing into mirrors. 'Who was she with, then? Some short arse. Your uncle Malcolm got together with her friend. Meg…? Can't bastard remember.'

'You met *mum* in there?'

I'd gone nightclubbing a few times with my mum, for my sins, in my teens. Not at The Ritzy, scene of parental coupling, but at Croydon's Blue Orchid. It was with my sister too, plus a few of my mum's work friends from payroll at Nestlé, the town's very own dark Satanic mill. I was the token male those evenings to fend off the advances of idiots but also scarper in the advances of handsome chaps, and if party to a female advance, my embarrassment provided light entertainment amongst the permed payrollers. If I'd been a more confident kid, I would have made the most of learning from this group of women. I was too shy to do so; but I was comfortable too, inside the matronly coven. And anyway, I didn't want to disturb the peace, and generally sank into my lager and limes and watched the girls go by.

Dad wrinkled his nose. At the memory of meeting her, my mum? Were his eyes watery? Was he reminiscing that they had been young once, and fancied each other, not knowing what was to come or having yet pressed upon each other's wounds, as they propped up the bar or danced to rock and roll and drank whisky and maybe went home together?

'Did you—how long did you date?'

'She was pregnant in the year,' he said, 'with Kelly. Your sister.'

There is a photograph—I don't have many, less than half a dozen—of my dad in one of his trademark patterned Debenhams jumpers sitting on a sofa holding my newborn sister in his drunken arms. His hair was already receding, wisping across his head. He'd not been at the birth, not in those days, but down The Star waiting for the call. She'd been like all babies, my sister: small, pink, fresh with the possibilities of life. How brief it all is. Four years later he'd be gone with the other woman (who became our stepmother), and she'd be wailing (my sister; thirty years later our stepmother too) because she'd been old enough to understand he was leaving. I, a two-year-old, blamed for spilling the gravy at the Sunday dinner table, an act known in family mythology as *the final straw*, was too young to remember. I understood less, maybe wailed less too. And yet I still *carried preverbal trauma* (said my therapist). Of course. But I'd had the luck to be clever, and entered the socioeconomic category that had access to *inner work*. I was to balance my Adverse Childhood Experiences on the scales of therapy and learn to put the weight down, gravy boat an' all. Which my sister had never done, and which, as with our mum, had stayed inside her, manifesting not as story but obesity and, in the end, the unshed weight did for them both.

I didn't know what else to ask about that fateful night at the Cat's Whiskers.

'I never knew that,' was all.

He sucked his teeth.

'Couldn't bastard trust her either, so you say,' he said to keep the pleasant conversation going. I frowned. Turned left again, towards Clapham Common. I didn't ask what he meant until we'd made it to Battersea Power Station and the Thames was in view.

'What do you mean?'

'Wha?'

'Couldn't trust mum?'

'Nah, nahimbaemae.'

'*What?*' I wasn't having his tonal tuneout.

'Ah, it doesn't fucking matter.' But then, as if it did, 'not by what you said.'

Ah. When I first turned up at his door (surprise!) although we didn't speak much, I did update him about things he'd missed in the intervening fifteen years. One, being my mum had died. His wife of that handful of years four decades earlier, the mother of his two children, who he'd abandoned once she was no longer the cat's whiskers. He'd been sorry then about her death, and it felt genuine. (He was never *only* bitter. In fact, I remembered more demonstrations of love from my father than my mother. The problem being the *demon* in demonstration.) I can't remember exactly how I told him what came next but it probably started *I don't think she ever got over the trauma and it killed her* and he'd pushed out his gummy underbite thinking it an attack; that is, I was unnecessarily highlighting the trauma of his walking out on her to struggle alone with two kids. But *no, I mean* I meant *the trauma of having to give up her first child for adoption when she got pregnant at seventeen.* His eyes widened and I thought, *I've just told my dad his first wife had a kid before they met.* (Hence my doubt at his feigned shocks, or his story about the African virus, or not knowing how Google works—I fucking know what surprise looks like, daddio.) And *his* shock, even at that moment, was not a surprise to *me*, knowing my mother. She didn't tell us, her kids, that she'd had a child before us—not until our half-sister came knocking and it was difficult to explain away this younger spitting image of our mum at the front door (another surprise!). Poor mum. I don't think she ever got over the catastrophe of giving up her first born. She carried it like a sack of kittens as she grew older and heavier and crumblier and finally died of an arthritic spine and organ failure. We'd probably *never* have known if our half-sister's adoptive parents hadn't told her of her origins, when at least one cat, whiskers intact, was let right out of the bag.

'I think it's more complicated than that,' back to the conversation, defending mum *in absentia*. Thinking, *we're on the way to my fucking sister's funeral. Your daughter's funeral.* Thinking, *oh*, my half-sister would be there too. That was going to be an interesting encounter.

He shrugged. I sighed. Lid of the can closed, for now.

*

We rounded onto Westminster Bridge and traffic was at a grind. What was Google playing at? This was taking us across Parliament Square. I guessed the other possible routes were worse. It was midmorning Monday, after all.

'I guess the other routes are worse,' I pre-empted his critique. I pointed at the phone. 'Google Maps. It's always calculating the fastest route.'

He post-empted my pre-empt with a laugh and shake of the head.

'Not doing a very good job. I dunno why people trust those fucking things.'

'I never minded using real maps.'

'Who drives through central London? Should've gone left.'

I stifled a huff. *Should 'a done a lot of things.* He nodded, which, bearing in mind I thought I'd said it in my head, raised the spectre he had pre-cognitive access to the universal field too. My father the telepath. Maybe I'd inherited it? Or did I actually say that out loud?

'What's going on?' he said, pointing with his underbite.

'Hey?'

'Over there. In our way.'

I chewed the inside of my cheek but he was right, and I hadn't noticed (so not telepathic). We were driving into something. Bugger. A march, protest, something disruptive outside Parliament. I couldn't see properly as we were behind a truck bed of scaffolding poles. Shit it! But we weren't going to be late. We had time. We inched forward. I'd had the radio on low for background distraction but now switched it off. I could hear shouting, whistles, a steel band. Another inch. Another. We were almost alongside Big Ben but there was no right turn, so we'd have to go left (*got your way, daddio!*) and through whatever it was, although, knowing a thing or two about protests, I figured the main body of people would be on the grass, with the police keeping the road clear. Across Parliament Green there were hundreds of protesters, but something about them was not coalesced. I kept stealing glances as we inched forward, through the flags and tents that flapped at the front of the Green and a line of police flanking my side of the road. I could make out a hazy divide. On the right your typical protesters: a jumble of banners, some colourful costumes, megaphones, a puce tuk-tuk carting a sound system, the Hari Krishna food trolleys, and countless white people in Berghaus jackets with flasks and backpacks. Then, on the left, what looked like an 80s football crowd in bomber uniforms. Shit. Fascists. Fash, as they were called by people who knew. Formerly the National Front or UKIP, then the dregs of Reform, and now the contemporary *fashista,* a pride of balding white men (and the odd, very odd, Asian female MP) in buttoned-up Fred Perry polo shirt waving pseudo-Nazi flags.

And then down the middle of the divide came a line of forty dancing badgers.

The Badger Liberation Army.

'What the hell?'

Dad was snorting phlegm in conjecture. I gagged.

'Fash,' I said. And feeling the need to explain further, 'Fascists. There, look,' pointing.

That's when it broke out. I could feel it, even in the car, the switchup of energy. Spiky all of a sudden, perilous. The police rank through which we'd been watching the scene scrambled, both into and away from the fighting. Every car stopped its inching dead as the melee flooded between traffic. Everywhere I looked there was fighting, some of the fumbling kind, and others nasty, the police involved in their militarised luminous bulk, pulling people away and getting the odd thump in return.

'Jesus Christ.' Dad this time.

Almost on top of us, one angry Fash caught a Berghaus-clad protestor by the straps of his backpack and started to thump his head. Then a badger was upon them, a costumed black and white mask with a papier-mâché snout swinging a powerful right paw into the Fash's face. Blood from his nose spattered over the car bonnet.

'Gordon Bennett,' was all I could manage. My insides were frigid.

On my dad's side a bunch of scared middle-Englanders were edging away from the centre being followed, spat at, things thrown at, by four or five of the fascists.

'Get my crutches,' my dad said.

It didn't compute. 'What?'

He pushed the car door open to block the path of the advancing Fash.

'I don't—' but what didn't I? What? I leant into the back to pull the crutches through to the front but clattered myself in the face, so dropped them and opened my door and got out then back in to get the car key just in case a Fash opportunist saw them, and then ran round to the passenger side and got the crutches out. I helped my dad up and fed his arms into the callipers and then he was leaning on his open door, holding a crutch so it reached the car alongside, blocking the path between Fash and the retreating protesters. In his World Darts Championship shirt he looked like a cross between Jocky Wilson and a car park barrier.

'Fucking cunt,' one of the Fash said, with a vicious jab of a finger at my dad, and gave the car door a bit of a boot. It didn't move much. I was holding the door too, and my dad wavered but was propped up by his other crutch. The Fash could easily have pushed the makeshift barrier out of the way, but then maybe even somewhere in a fascist's blistered heart you don't sweep the crutches out from under the disabled. It probably helped that both my dad and I looked a bit like them—white men with paunches and little hair. The five Fash jiggled with aggression and there was a lot of spittle. Then something caught my eye so I looked over the Fash's domed scalps, which reminded me of those eggs I didn't eat and the reproductive suffering of hens, to see coming towards us a couple of badgers. The Fash saw me looking and turned.

'Fucking cunts!' one Fash screamed as the badgers were on their backs, swinging into them with wooden sticks that had not long before, I imagined, held *Stop the Badger Cull!* placards. I gasped as the handles thwacked the hemmed-in and cowering far-righties who were trying to defend themselves with bomber-sleeved arms, which was when my dad went further rogue and started thwacking the Fash over the head with his raised crutch. Crack! Like smashing the head of Humpty Dumpty. Crack! I couldn't actually laugh, although that was the sound that wanted to come out of me, after the gasping, out of panic. I couldn't reach to land a punch so I held the door firm, with the scene evoking a memory of my stepmother taking off her stiletto and cracking it down onto the heads of my mates who had started a massive fight at the denouement of my (cuntydoorframe) birthday party. (Says something when the defining memory of my father from my 18th was not, in fact, his sweary drunken self-pity, but rather when I had to drag the hardest kid in school, Carl Popovic, off my dad as he lay floundering like an upturned turtle in the front garden. Anyway, back to the Fash.)

Then the two badgers were away, just as four police officers grabbed the first people they could, two cops on one Fash each, thrust to the ground with elbows bent behind their backs. The other Fash rushed past my dad's left crutch, which had returned to barrier position. But the escapees were not trying to get after the retreating protesters, who had anyway gotten well clear, but simply to run the fuck off as fast as possible from the PoPo.

The hapless Fash arrestees bumped up against the open car door, making one of the officers look up at us. 'Get back in the car, sirs,' he said.

I moved to help my dad.

'Nah, nahimbaemae,' he shrugged me off, waving the crutch. Was there blood on the end? For the first time I fixed eye contact with the driver of the car stopped alongside us; there were smudgy crutch prints on his driver-side window. He was probably halfway the age between my father and myself, white Oxford cotton collar under a jumper, and in the passenger seat was a woman of the same age with short grey-brown hair. Their eyes were wide in shock, with none of the... exaltation and pride. Yes, I suppose it was those things I felt. None of the exaltation and pride in their faces that were flushing through me.

We stood for a bit, the traffic going nowhere. The police pulled the two Fash off the ground and away, bundling them into wagons. Two protesters passed and I stopped them to discover the details of how it had all started. Apparently, it was a fascist march against the government for not stopping the small boats as they'd promised, spouting bollocks about the threat of 'Critical Race Theory' and the deteriorating fates of the white working class, boys in school being outclassed by Pakistanis and Muslims, according to the Fash anyway (I didn't know they read *The Telegraph*). The anti-fascist collaboratives, from trades unions, Antifa, Extinction Rebellion and the like, had turned up, like they tended to, to drown out the racism and offer protection for any minorities who stumbled into the alt-right path.

'And the badgers?' I asked.

'An accident, apparently,' said the protester I was talking to, an Aussie guy with a big smile and a topknot. 'They were protesting the Badger Cull outside Defra,' and he waved a hand off to the far corner of Parliament Green, 'and got wind something was going on.'

'Fascist cunts!' laughed the other protester, a woman with multicoloured hair whom I noted was wearing a white jacket with the word 'RESIST' in bold letters down one arm. 'Bloody love badgers.'

They left then, and my dad handed me his crutches as he fumbled himself into the passenger seat. I threw the sticks into the rear footwell and got in myself. I opened my window, wanting to soak up more of the atmosphere. Though it had peaked and was now fizzling out, it still held something unusual, rare, and—now, at least, the fight was over—comforting. I didn't know what it was exactly, I couldn't quite—and then I could—It was winning. No, not winning exactly. It was being asked to show your best and delivering. Even though we hadn't meant to be part of something, we had been, and, for the first time in decades, since perhaps Monday Night Darts down The Star, it had been a dad-and-I arrangement. It gave us something that we hadn't been able to generate for ourselves for a long time: a *we* in which neither of us disappointed the other.

We could've stayed longer. Parked the car and proudly joined the mopping up, the energetic inquest of the victors. Got a selfie with the badgers. But we had a funeral to get to. Even so, I wondered if the heat of battle would loosen things, as unexpected shared moments can. Maybe we'd chat about what we'd just seen, about my dad's impressive courage, about badger vaccination, my work with climate activists, the marches he'd joined as a youngster in Glasgow to protest the nuclear submarines based in Faslane, the CND charm and chain he said he'd worn back then. I drove norther into London heading for the circular. We didn't talk—my dad's dangerous breathing returned—but in the interludes between rattling I imagined my dad having taken a different lane, as not an apprentice engineer but a campaigner, not a drunk with broken marriages but a middle-class manager holding together a life, a story. Someone who hadn't stumbled upon but had *meant to be* at the protest. Had taken his family. Even wore a Berghaus jacket (like mine!) and carried a backpack and flask (of tea, not whisky). A different wife, different children. Even so, I could imagine, couldn't I? It wasn't too late for that?

'Yeah, I remember,' he said finally.

I wondered, again, if he was reading my mind. Remembered that other life? Remembered who my mum's friend was that night in the Cat's Whiskers? Oh, remem—

'"*Shoulda' called you Judas*",' he gurgled, a mode of his phlegmy broken laughter.

That's what he'd said when I'd shown him my G.C.S.E.s.

For getting an A* in Religious Studies, which hadn't been an option but compulsory given it was a Catholic school. And despite my other As and A-stars and two years of hard study, that was *all* he said. I'd been at his place, it being a Saturday and that was the alimony agreement for dividing up our time as kids. He'd been leaning on the three-quarter height fridge in his kitchen that led off from the living room, and I was sat on the sofa next to the tropical fish tank he kept full of guppies, neon tetras and bottom-eating catfish (which used to make me giggle: bottom-eating!). '*Shoulda' called you Judas*' he'd said, and left my results on the fridge top and opened its door and pulled out a can of Heineken.

He was chuckling to himself now, as if it had been a joke. I realised that over the passing years he'd moulded the memory so that it *had* been a joke, in his recall; as if he could never have been such a fucking bastard to mean it for real. *Judas*. But no. He knew he'd meant it for real; otherwise why invite me, only a few years later, to call him *call me a cunt*? As a joke, it was one of the cruellest. So it hadn't been. And I was too old now for this, too wearied by his self-fooling revisionism. It could hardly be dismissed as a one-off in a childhood of otherwise loving bliss, could it?

'You're laughing. You thought it was funny?'

'It was a joke.'

'No it wasn't.'
'Are you telling me what I meant?'
'I thought your memory was shot?'
'Nah,' he began. *Don't say it!* 'Nahimbaemae.'
'It wasn't funny,' I whispered and drove on. We weren't even at the North Circular.
But it was too late now anyway.
'At least you didn't become a priest,' he said after a while.
'I did something right?'
But no. Too late.

*

My sister's *every bone in her body* was revisionism too. Maybe dad had done *something*—not *that* though—and it evolved into a story that my sister repeated to people like Tracy, to help explain away the gaps in her life. Unless it *had* happened. But then I wouldn't have been born—no marriage could survive *that*, could it? He would've been locked up. Of course I was only a baby, so... so, no. The damage done by our father had been wrought through words, anger, the *demon*strations in alcoholic abusings, unpredictability. Not overwhelming physical violence. It was a shame for them both, that they never spoke. In making things up, they were very familiar.

A passing fantasy had me request an autopsy on my sister's bones from a forensic palaeontologist's lab to reveal the secrets of her skeleton. However, in the field of real things, as far as I understood it, my sister's death had arrived not from *osteofuckuparentis*, but while having a caramel latte on the promenade, near her beloved pier arcade and the seafront kiosk that sold cod and tripled-fried chips. She'd smelled of caramel and cream until the funeral director got a clean set of clothes from the grieving Gavin so others could visit her in the chapel of rest (no hot drinks allowed). She did love the waterfront. After their Town Hall civil wedding six months earlier, the bridal party had decamped to the pier bar (outdoor heaters for the vapers and a lovely sea view) and then into the arcades to spend tuppences on the shoving machines, winning a handful of teddies, pink plastic watches and mini buckets of sugar for the kids. I'd drifted around, avoiding the others, to be honest, with no other family of my own in attendance (Aunt and Uncle had not approved of the pier). It was mainly the groom's family, who I'd never met (no Gavin's dad either, incidentally). I went looking for retro arcade machines, games I used to play as a kid when we went on family holidays with our dad down to the caravan park at Selsey Bill. Back then my favourite was *Mr Do!*, (ah! Maybe that's where all the ! come from), a Japanese classic similar to Pac-man, where the player has to eat all the cherries in the bushes while running from the Oompa Loompa ghosties. I became good at it, which stretched out the week's £5 spending money, games back then (the early 80s) being 10p per play. The caravan park arcade was an escape from the three-quarters empty cabaret, the Yard of Ale competitions, my stepmother's Mai-Tai cocktails with plastic monkey charms hanging over the rim, my father's pints of Tennants Pilsner, and the utter fear-induced boredom of not being able to, well, *be*. Another memory flash: my stepmother's older son and his friends poking fun at my puppy fat, likening me to famous 80s American Footballer William 'The Refrigerator' Perry, who played for the Chicago Bulls. Perry was a huge man, obese, at the time a sporting anomaly. I was christened the 'Ice Box' as a mini-Perry and I ran off in tears. (Did they not understand A.C.Es, my step-brother's friends? Obesity is trauma, boys!) Anyway, my father followed and berated me: *you should be able to take a bit of ribbing*. Adding *if you can find them!* (my ribs) and maybe I *maybe you should lose some weight*. I remember, even as a seven-year-old attempted runaway, thinking,

But how *do you lose weight, daddio?* How?

Same old story. It was more useful for him to blame our (overweight) mum for her poor parenting than to address the problem in which he may well have had a hand.

Anyway, my sister. I don't remember spending time with her on those childhood holidays. Except one moment: we were both wearing t-shirts in the packed swimming pool, ostensibly to protect our sunburn but, I think we both knew, to hide our rolls of fat. This bodily shame did for everything. It spread out to smother our relationship as brother and sister. I barely remembered having her as a sibling in childhood, least of all during the visits with our father. The divorce, and the previously mentioned alimony agreement, specified that each Saturday we'd go to our dad's. From 10am to 6pm we'd wait out the day in famine and fear, ashamed of being hungry or asking even for a drink in case it brought attention to our bodies. The time slot was devastating, as my favourite TV programmes—*The A-Team, Knight Rider, Chips*—were, for reasons I've never understood, scheduled to run in the inexplicable 5.35-6.30pm slot. We'd inevitably miss the central development of the storyline as our dad rushed to drive us home to our mum bang on time. Why our parents couldn't negotiate a 5.30pm or 6.30pm end zone was not a question we thought to touch down upon. Anyway: my sister and her absence sitting there next to me through the bleak years. Did I look away from her fatness for fear it mirrored my own? Have I cut her from my memories like a cuckold might the cheating lover from family photos? Does this forgetfulness of sibling intertwinement naturally happen as we age, especially when one of you is dead? Who knows? Yet the idea that we could be allies when with our dad—my enemy's enemy is my friend, etc.—never occurred to us, and we rarely played together, and barely talked when we did. Did I even know what my sister liked? What she thought? Not much. Fermented in the vat of embodied disgrace, there had congealed fibrotic wedges between us from an early age. Potentially older sibling jealousy was involved, of course, on her side, towards this baby who came along and upset the gravy boat, pulled the *final straw* and hastened my dad's exit. Or was it that as kids our choices in film (*Sound of Music* vs. *Star Wars*) and music (Madonna vs. Phil Collins) were too unalike for sharing? Or that I shed the fat (mostly) and she did not. Or that being loving to each other meant to bear the threat of the loss of *that* love, too. Perhaps I became, no doubt, the annoying brother who was school smart, had some confidence (opposed to her negative indices) and, as the boy in a patriarchal world, received more leeway to make mistakes. And I don't doubt my father found it easier to spend time with a son than a daughter—a son you could take to The Star, for example, almost exclusively men. And I, an introspective character, found more cavities in which to secrete the shames that our father rent upon us. I also had more reasons to stick with my father, as my sister sucked up the available affection from our mother, as well as the full platform of solidity offered by our maternal grandfather. If I didn't have my dad, I'd have no-one. Which in the end, I did.

I didn't find *Mr Do!* in the pier arcade after my sister's wedding. But while contemplating the three-person Mario Kart machine, my sister surprised me from behind, *Want a game?* and of course it was her wedding so I said yes, and I, she, and her new husband Gavin raced each other on Mario Kart (I won) before they then wandered one way and I another, and the brief moment of connection throwing upturned turtle shells to bounce each other's karts off the track, came to a close. So we hadn't disowned each other, my sister and I, as she had our dad. But we lived distant lives and barely spoke, with communication coming through a third party, Auntie, our mum's sister. It was this aunt who'd informed me that my sister had her heart attack, and despite the defibrillator hanging on the pier wall 50 feet away—a foot for every year of her life—she hadn't recovered consciousness and died at the scene. Whaleish, pink, irrevocably caramelised by a last latte before death.

'I got it wrong,' I told my dad. I rubbed my stubble, hiding my face somewhat. 'We're not actually going on the North Circular.'

'I could 'a told you that.'

'Hmm.' *Could 'a*, but *did'nae*. 'Crossing it. We're heading straight out on the A12.'

'Yep.'

Rub the chin, hold the tongue. My new mantra!

I checked the estimated arrival time: another two hours, the numerals in orange, which meant somewhere a motoring delay. But! Musing on my sister's life, something had clicked. I knew, suddenly, that the sore words stored in my hippocampus from childhood would always be worse—internalised by a child—than anything a live performance from Mr CuntyDoorFrame could do to me as an adult. I'd *proved* that when I'd turned up to surprise him after fifteen years. I'd been present, in control, the Capital-A Adult in the room. So I sat up straight in my driving seat, rearranged my bum, checked my mirrors before manoeuvres, set myself to speak. Hadn't I just seen him at his best—taking on five Fash—and relished it? Weren't we both men now? Wasn't I being silly thinking I couldn't handle opening the can? Wasn't there a hope to throw it open to the light, unbury it all?

'I got it wrong.'

'You said that already,' he chided me, shaking his head. Disappointed! *You fucker!* But Capital-A. Come on, son.

'If you'd turned left, we'd be round the M25 by now,' he added.

I looked across at him and shook my head.

'No, actually, because I knew the JSO protesters were out today.'

'The who?'

'Just Stop Oil. The climate protesters. Blocking the M25.'

'That lot.'

His arms folded on his paunch as if he'd won a debate.

'Yes, that lot.'

'Just Shove Off.'

'Oh, very good.' To be fair, his word puzzles were staving off the dementia. But then, 'it's the same as you were doing when you were on those CND marches, isn't it?'

'Fucking no. That was different. It was the Cold War.'

'I know what war.'

'So it's fucking different, innit.'

'I bet people said the same about CND back then. About you. Called you extremists.'

That got him. Must've been true. He pushed out his bottom lip.

'Why did you feel so strongly about it?' I asked him. 'CND? To go and march?'

He shrugged, like he couldn't remember, or it was too painful to go that far back. Maybe because it was the same thoughts and fantasy I'd had earlier. He *could* have lived a different life, taken that different lane. Maybe there was a girl he'd met on the march into Faslane. They'd shared a banner, hands touched, swapped stories, lost her when the police piled in.

'That was nuclear holocaust. They were gonna blow the world up.'

'Still blowing the world up, just more slowly. With oil, not missiles.'

'Is that what they think, is it? Pissing off drivers on the way to work is doing what?'

'Half an hour ago you were an anti-fascist. You were a protester.'

'Nah, I was just—'

'Just what? Just stopping…?'

'Nah, nahimbaemae.'

'Hmm.'

A pause in the repartee as we drove past Hornchurch, and another memory: I came here once as a young teenager, to a model shop, the kind that sold Airfix planes and trains and those small cans of Humbrol enamel that were as full of enigma as they were paint. I came to Hornchurch on the Tube, the longest journey I'd made on my own aged fourteen. I felt both the freedom of it and the terror. And the shame, always the shame, which I carried through my childhood like rocks in a backpack; no room in the pack for much else, such as the joyful anticipation of buying the 1932 Ford Model B kit I'd come for, so full it was, this carrier bag of shame that I, shame the shop owner would, shame the other kids with their dads might… full'a bricks of shame. A cruciform kinda shame: a hypervigilance of attending to the emotions of others and what they thought of me, always expecting the worst. Another look, another rock: chuck it in the backpack! Wonder where that habit came from, hey daddio?

I tried making the Ford Model B kit, 1:32 scale, but I wasn't very dextrous and never a perfectionist. Like most things I tried as a child—the piano lessons, the woodwork, the football—I gave up too soon as the panopticon gaze of my dad landed on me, even when he wasn't there. The Ford Model B kit, 1:32 scale, was aborted, shoved away at the back of the wobbly wardrobe with the wee-stained pyjamas. JSO. Just Shame, Obviously.

'How's you know?'

'What?'

I floated back to the car. Hornchurch receding into the past as we went under the M25.

'How's you know that lot would be on the M25?'

'I help them. I do a lot of work for the climate, dad.'

Which you *would* know, if you had googled me.

'I see.'

The fuck—. Capital-A. CAPITAL-A!

I shook my head.

'They're mostly kids. And they're terrified of the future. You lot burnt all the gas and—' but looking at him, he never enjoyed the boom years, did he? He spent them dousing his wounds with eighty proof. And to be fair, again, his later career, you could say, as a recycler of heavy industry fixing broken engines, had saved thousands of tons of CO_2 from going into the manufacture of new parts. The Thompson Engineering factory repaired faulty metal, not for cars but cruise liners and other seafaring behemoths. The off-centre camshafts of ship's engines, like massive almonds on telegraph poles, would arrive on double-length Artex lorries and be winched into the factory and laid on my dad's lathe, a fifty-foot bench where my dad, a skilled labourer, would correct the cam wobble by adding and then grinding away new metal, sending the shaft back to sea. Done with pride. The issue with the climate crisis, as I saw it at least, was not actually the lobbyists or denialists or false hope or doomerism or helplessness or misplaced optimism. It was that we didn't know how to handle lost pride. The engineers, coalminers, the people who powered 20th century Britain, and were proud of it, taught to be proud of it, didn't react well to being told they'd been the problem all along. *But we didn't know!* No, they didn't. They raised their kids and enjoyed the boom. They forged national renewal after a punishing world war. No fucking point criticising them for it now. (Unless they worked for an oil company.

They knew. They *could* Just Shove Off.) And all British politicians did now was mismanage the country's pride, generally without steel enough in their own personalities to avoid it corroding into vanity (Exhibit 1: The BoJo). The newspapers and the right wing think tanks were constantly evoking and provoking pride—usually pride lost. Unless we channelled the primal need of human beings—*men*, of course—to feel pride, into other things, into healthier expressions of national interest, then we'd not avoid collapse and heat death. And the *national* interest was always made up of *people's* interests, and people's interests were, as I saw it, avoiding pain (the can!), securing the cave, and exhibiting pride.

I considered if I'd given my dad's pride enough attention. How he felt, his son turning up after fifteen years and seeing him *doddery old fucker* in the state he was. How he felt with his daughter *don't bring that bastard* disowning him, his family not searching for him when lost (even though we had, sort of). It was pride that made him lie about not knowing how Google worked. Pride that—

'Glad I fucking no drive no more,' he interrupted my train. He was staring down at his feet to emphasise the reasons. It somehow made me smell them, his bandaged tootsies, the iron tang of dried blood and god knows what mucosal and medicinal decoction. Urgh.

'Anyway,' I changed the subject. For some reason I felt less fear now of the can; rather, opening the can while sat beside him (driving the excuse for not looking his way) seemed the easiest opportunity I'd ever get. And I had a hypothesis to play with,

What were you proud of, dad? So...

'What are you going to say to her husband?' I asked. 'When we get there. I told you he... So I don't know how he's going to react. He's a complete softy, really. Harmless. A bit of an idiot and he's got his comics and OCD so I don't know... Gavin doesn't really drink so you can't sit at the bar with him and settle your differences. I'm guessing there'll be a bar. It's probably at the pier, the wake. Just thought... you know...'

Capital-A Adult trailed off. But it was a start.

He sunk into the passenger seat for a while, chewing (quite

literally) over my words. We were still on the A12, approaching the delightful windmills of Mountnessing.

'What differences?'

'Hey?'

'You said "settle our differences"? What differences? I've never fucking met him.'

In-terest-ing. Tell the truth, or—but I suppose there was no *or* any more.

'I guess he's inherited the differences. From Kels.'

My sister, Kelly. No one called her Kelly though. Apart from dad.

The hurt was visible on his face whenever we spoke about my sister, and I didn't want to continue. But then he'd hurt her. Even if *every broken bone* was metaphorical. Well, it was, absolutely. It was the fabulistic manifestation of a daughter who looked up to and adored her father, before being ripped from his breast and discarded as he ran off with another woman. But she was not here now (my sister) and he was, and in my charge. And without wanting to sound like a TikTok meme: no healing without hurting! It would be a relief for him, too, surely, to have those wounds exposed, given tincture, and wrapped with new bandages? Painful, but no more than having chewed-up feet.

We were past Mountnessing and into Margaretting now, as if this part of Essex was all suffix. On either sides of us long stretches of autumning trees offered glimpses of once common land through their shedding branches. Ah, time for poetry. Time still. Not too late.

'What differences then?' he asked, in a tone I'd not heard before.

Ah, but in fact *had* heard, *once* before: when I was six years old, as he apologised for his rage in the Tomato Sandwich Incident. This was on holiday at a place called Selsey Bill, in one of the static caravans. As a kid I wondered what made Bill so Selsey, but was never brave enough to enquire... I was too young then for *Mr Do!* and the arcades. One day for lunch I'd been asked if I wanted tomato in my cheese sandwich. Did I like tomato? *Like* tomato? I didn't even *know* tomato. I was too afraid to admit I didn't know.

So I'd just nodded. And found, after all, that no, I *did not much like tomato*, and definitely not how it made white bread all soggy. I couldn't eat it. My father snapped, shouted, raged. Over tomato. The Incident became a ruddy burnish on the mind's eye, to surface decades later in therapy and visions summoned by a Peruvian shaman. The Incident had been long-injurious, and finally healed by the hard (bloody hard) work of the Capital-A adult through *inner work*: expunging the squelchy tomato tomato tomato! He'd cried, my dad, while apologising, knowing that his extended, caravan-confined, plate-shattering rage at six-year-old me, gagging on soggy white bread and cowering behind the laminate table of the dinette was, to put it mildly, an overreaction. Explaining his rage a few years later when I was fifteen, as we walked back a little drunk from The Star, he said it (the rage) had been caused (of course) by me (who else!) because, get this, I was *a child of hate*. That hadn't soothed my Inner Child much, I can tell you. *I hated your mum*, he'd said to me, and *your mum hated me, so I got her pregnant to ruin her career*, and then the unlikely shift of blame to *she tried to suffocate you with a pillow*. After many years of the *inner work,* or indeed wondering if I'd heard it wrong, even on the odd occasion asking *was it true? had mum, in her post-partum pain, tried to suffocate me?*, I put his excuses for the raging tomato outburst down to *his* tendency to make things up, to explain away *his* painful gaps (the jettisoning, etc.) through projection, that old chestnut (or indeed, lycopersicum).

It was, I noted, the same predisposition as practiced—inherited—by my sister.

(What differences? No fucking differences, if you asked me.)

'Well,' I began, getting back to the present and his question. *Softly...* 'She never quite... She never left home, you know, Kels. She never really had the chance to grow—up, I mean. Become independent. Okay, she married. Gavin. But he's a child too. Not all the time. But, you know... I don't think she was ever able to...'

Hmm. This was hard. I saw we were now driving past Crix, and crix was how it felt.

'Look...'

To come after Crix it was Feering, Messing, and Ardleigh. You couldn't make it up!

I wasn't sure he was listening anyway to my stumbling analysis. It didn't inspire confidence in the telling. Why was I being so uncertain? Surely he was readier to hear it now than he'd ever been? But I wasn't sure I was readier to say it. How to tell him it was his fault without telling him it was his fault?

We drove on in a silence that lasted all the way between Ardleigh and Dedham.

'Yeah, she never got in touch with me either,' he said out of Dedham Vale (look it up if you don't believe me), a semblance of sorrow, and then after a pause, 'and I don't know why.'

I don't know why. I DON'T KNOW WHY! Christ.

'Christ,' I said, and although I said it for another reason—my phone screen, and the map, had just that second gone blank—he clearly thought I was responding to his wonderment at my sister disowning him.

'What, you fucking think you do know why?'

His sorry tomatoey tone was squished, alright.

'Yes,' was all I said, and I think it was the bravest thing I'd ever said, and then ruined it, as it wasn't all I said, as I said, 'maybe' to follow. I glanced across; his anger was deflating. His cheeks sunken into his gums. He wasn't drunk enough to sustain it, I guess. Or just too old, and on his way to a funeral. *Mine too, you know! My sadness too!* 'You left us. She was properly old enough to remember it. She was scared.'

'Scared? Of what.'

'We both were,' I said, redirecting. 'We never knew—you were... The drink. *"Shoulda' called you Judas"*...? They weren't nice things to say—I don't know what you said to her.'

'No say nothing to her,' slipping into Scots, into childhood. 'Anyway, that was a joke.'

He giggled again.

'"*Judas*" was a *joke?*'

Actually giggled.

'Not to a sixteen-year-old it wasn't.' And the tomato. 'Not to a frightened six-year-old.'

I loosened my knuckles on the steering wheel. I could hear my heart. My heart sac had ruptured when I was a kid falling out of our garden plum tree and landing on a half-buried brick. I'd suffered pericarditis since. But my heart—my strong heart, actually, many times tested—was unusually loud in my chest ever after. It worried people (girlfriends resting their cheeks on my cavity, strangers in quiet waiting rooms). It worried me now.

'I just don't know why,' he repeated, and there he went! Gone. To the same inner sanctum the drink took him, clearly accessible without booze when under duress.

I don't know why, hey!

He'd said the exact same thing when I'd taken him for a drink that *two cream doughnuts* time. *I don't know why.* I'd sat there then, just as I was sitting there in the car driving, feeling most of all sadness, for him and her. Sadness that neither of the pair ever felt they had the option of therapy, to expose their wounds and have them dressed. Sadness that neither could see who they were: hurt adults, yes, but with the right to be loved by each other. He was a seventy-six-year-old child, or rather, a ten-year-old child who'd been jettisoned by his parents, African virus and all. He'd never had the chance to grow up (psychologically). By twelve he was smoking and drinking and by fourteen apprenticed in a factory surrounded by Glasgow's finest hard knockers. *I'd* had therapy; my wounds scarred over; healed the Inner Child. The wounds hadn't killed me like they killed her. (And were killing him.)

Yet I had other problems now. My phone was dead.

'But it's plugged in,' I muttered to myself, tracing the white cable from phone to cigarette socket. 'Bloody... it must be faulty.'

I knew to take the A14, but we'd have to ask directions for the rest.

'Can you play with the wires, see if it's loose?'

He turned towards me, sending across a waft of musty clothes and stale bedsit. He pushed and pulled at the wire but nothing lit up. It would be okay. I remembered the name of the funeral parlour. If not, I was sure the crematorium would be signposted, one of those brown signs for civic institutions and National Trust buildings. It was out of town somewhere and I didn't know exactly where, but we'd find it.

'We'll ask someone,' I said.

'Someone old,' he said.

I looked across, quizzical, thinking *Let's Get Quizzical*, probably the best quiz team name of all time, which H had come up with, and I felt a terrible pang of loneliness, and regret, knowing it would have been so much easier to deal with my dad if she'd been here, a loving partner, good with people, a willing buffer. If we'd still been together. But I hadn't dealt with all my wounds back then when we'd been together, before I'd been through thera—

'They'll know where the fucking funerals are.'

'Old people?' I got it. 'Ah, old people.'

'Aye.'

'How many you been to?' I asked. 'Funerals.'

'Not enough,' he said, and laughed. He caught me there. I shook my head, blinking. You'd expect the opposite from polite company, but then he didn't like polite much. People. No, not true. He *did* like people, but protected himself from that vulnerability by being sour and difficult; impolite. Aha! Insight: the *more* he liked them, loved them, the greater lengths he went to protect himself from them. Marvellous! But bless (which means *sprinkled with blood*, let's not forget), yes, bless him, he'd simply passed onto *us* what had been done to *him*, right? I reminded myself again: abandonment by an alcoholic parent is an Adverse Child Experience, daddio! Because *his* alcoholic dad abandoned *him*, didn't he? The Glasgow Jettison—a natural-industrial phenomenon, like London Smog. But yes, Grandad Bill of the Coldstream Guards (*not* Selsey Bill, to avoid that misunderstanding) the grandfucker, also an alcoholic. And Grandfather Bill's dad, did *his* alcoholic dad abandon him? Was there a Greatgrandfucker? And a greatgreatgrandfucker?

Upturned daddios all the way down.

I wished I could have said all this to him, my dad. Asked about all this. But I didn't. The can had somehow closed; after all that prying it had sprung back.

We journeyed on.

*

Okay, so

~~two cream doughnuts~~ = inner work leads to loving connection in the universal field,

~~his family~~ bastards, the lot of them,

~~my sister~~ *and I don't know why...*,

so: what he said about my book.

I gave him a copy of my previous book because, well, it's the kind of thing you do as a son with a father, isn't it? I didn't know if he'd read it. And what did I want anyway? Approval, sure. Something else? (Not a google review, obvs.) Bear in mind that at that moment in life, driving him to the funeral, I had not yet achieved my potential in life. This was in large part—my therapist will corroborate—owed to the fact that I'd grown up with *him*: an alcoholic, emotionally abusive father who abandoned us all when I was a babbio. And *also* bear in mind the reason that I was still, at forty-eight, single: was this also because I'd had a father whose main expression of emotion towards me was disappointment? But! Bear this in mind too: I *had* achieved things. A career, friends, inner healing. In sum: so, I did *not* give him the book *only* seeking assurance or praise. I was proud enough of it already (pride, see.) It was a good enough book. I offered it as a record of what I'd done in the intervening years since we'd mislaid each other. Anyway, he'd never read it, right?

He read it. And can you guess what he said?

Not bad, he said. What a moment that was! We were sitting at his kitchen table. I'd given him a bottle of whisky for his birthday, secretly hoping he'd open it and grease the moment for us both. He took up the book and flicked through. But all was still good. All was pleasant. Oh to have left it there! To have enjoyed it categorically; the book's themes were, after all, connected to the fantasy life I'd concocted for him in my head, and perhaps the fantasy life he had in his, had he CND-ed it and become a Berghaus-jacket-wearing campaigner and had different wives, different kids, but been happy. Happy.

No how I would 'a ended it.

'Pardon,' I think I'd replied.

Pardon?

'No how I would 'a ended it,' he'd repeated. 'I did'nae think he would do that, go and—'

Etc.

A recap: the central story of that book, by the way, was this: a brother, riven by family trauma and environmental disaster, finally faces up to the childhood issues that are stopping him living the life he wants. He ultimately overcomes his fears of telling the truth and does the right thing (as a whistleblower) and holds on to his marriage just in time, and reconciles with his estranged sister. What my dad *did'nae think he would do* (the novel's protagonist) was to accept his wrongdoings, then go and heal family trauma with said sister, before it was too late.

That is: my dad thought the protagonist wouldn't have the balls. He thought the protagonist was going to disappoint him! Oh, *Thalia* where are you now!

(BTW, when people pointed this out to me—*Oh you've written an autobiographical novel, it's about your relationship with your sister and fam*—I would stare at them blankly and ask, *Pardon? PARDON? What are you*—? So no, please don't. Don't email, or Tweet. I heed it, okay. *I heed it!*)

There it was: disappointment again. Daddio informing me, *my son the author*, had ended it the wrong way. My book! *My* book! Offering instead his own series finale of that sibling story.

But!

By the time daddio said *I did'nae think he would do that* I was retort-ready:

one) you had to find something to be disappointed in, didn't you?; and two) no, you couldn't imagine it, because *you* can't go and heal family trauma; *and*

three) at least I found some way to heal, even if it was through writing; and what is wrong with writing out your healing? Healing is, by its very nature, after the fact of a wounding. And writing is perhaps the post-factual exercise *par excellence* for digging up and exposing the factual wounds to the air; and, both the blessing and a curse of the fictional form, *daddio*, for better or worse, is that to heal is to finish the story, and to finish the story you have to choose an ending. The healing can't work otherwise. The un-finished story is an unhealed wound. And it was mine to choose. Mine, this time. Can you not just give me that, dad?

None of which I said to him, of course.

Which is why you're reading it, perhaps.

So, there you have it:

~~what he said about my book.~~

*

We were into the town. I knew the way to my sister's but I wasn't taking him there. I wondered if we might strike it lucky and pass the crematorium on the way, tending, as cemeteries and abodes of death do, to be on the outskirts. No one wants the smoke from cremations wafting through their neighbourhood. I'd just discovered aqaumation myself, and added it to my will; it was more expensive because rare, but a more environmentally friendly, less carbon-emitting form of returning to the earth. You get squished by fluid pressure, dissolved into fertiliser. You could probably argue my dad had started the trend sixty years early with a cheap and occasionally cheerful pickling process; if he *were* cremated, he'd go up like a flaming Sambuca. Aqaumation might be the safer process. Did anyone get buried anymore? Was that why we had less worms per square metre of soil, because they had less bodies to compost? Who knows. What I did know was I was avoiding the fact I didn't know where to go. For the first time since we'd left his bedsit in

London, I felt not only slightly sickened but also panicked.

'So what now?'

'Well. I was going to head to the funeral parlour and join the cavalcade. But—'

'The caval- what?'

'Cars. The cavalcade of cars.'

'Posh.' He shook his head. 'A posh conga.'

Piss off, I thought. Mind, he wasn't wrong. I imagined us doing the conga out of the crematorium following the ceremony, my dad thwacking the celebrant with his crutches.

'There can't be that many crematoriums,' I got us back on track.

'You'd be surprised,' he said, and I guess he'd seen a few go up in smoke in his years. He'd christened the flats either side of his 'The Pits' for having seen off seven and six, like an imperial grocer of death, seven in the bedsit on the left and six in the bedsit on the right, in his fourteen years. One or two he'd had a fling with, he told me, younger ladies (younger than him) who'd lost their husbands. I shivered to think what they made of his feet, but I guessed flings when you're in your seventies mostly involved tea dances (if you had the requisite equipment), card games, a bottle of spirits, and a Christmas nip under the mistletoe. I didn't want to imagine more, and thankfully couldn't. One of the women had survived the cursed bedsits and moved upstairs and found a more mobile man. My dad didn't begrudge her. He still got a birthday card from her and her fella each year. Pre-Covid, he'd told me, that pandemic we'd all forgotten about in the wake of the Greenland ice sheet crash and the food price rises that had sunk a few forgotten towns like this one already, yes, pre-pandemic there'd been quite a social life in sheltered housing. My dad enjoyed the company. He *did* like people. If it was on his terms—drinking—all the better. But the pandemic killed off more than care home residents. The social life of the shelter never rebounded; the lounge had sat empty since.

I was driving aimlessly now. Aimless felt uncomfortable.

'There,' he said, pointing with his chin then a wobbly hand.

'Where?'

'Bus stop. There's an old black fella. Stop and ask him.'

God. There *was* a person at the bus stop, but he was the *only* person, so mention of his skin colour was not necessary. (Anyway, not necessary any way!) I'd always been aware of my dad's casual racism, a flaw that, like the old catchphrase, *I've got loads of black friends,* was given cover by friendships with men he worked (but not socialised) with. Indian Peter (*COP'd* it!). There was also Udi, the Ugandan, the odd-job man around my father's factory, who I found, probably wrongly, a comic character because of his pidgin English and malapropisms, but also because he had a round face that seemed always smilingly troubled. Not least when he chopped off the high branch of a tree in the factory yard, the branch his ladder was resting on. I remembered one summer being called over to the pub to say goodbye to Udi, who had to go into hospital for an operation; never having been overnight in one before (hospital, not pub) he believed his time had come. I went across, he bought us two pints, we drank in silence, he gave me a nod and grunt like Mr Miagi in the *Karate Kid*, and I slipped off my stool to return to bending metals in the mezzanine of Thompson Engineering. (Udi survived. It was for gall stones.) But then my dad *would count the Pakis in* to the house opposite where he and my stepmother lived, always claiming there were seventy-odd benefit frauds packed in there. You didn't see a person of colour other than pinkie-white down The Star. It's not a solace to say that's what the 1970s were like, or that my father was only trying to fit in; my father was an enthusiastic carrier of generational racist banter and jokes at the immigrants' expense.

'Slow down,' I was instructed. The bus stop and the man were on my dad's side. Fuck, I hoped he didn't say something out of order. I was looking across. But trying not to crash meant I wasn't able to look with real attention; in my glances there seemed something odd about the man I couldn't quite put my finger on, and perhaps didn't want to, for my own fear of tripping over a desire not to be racist and putting my (nonnecrotized) foot right in it.

'What's he…?' *wearing*, I was to finish. But I didn't have time, we were indicating in.

'Hello!' my dad shouted out the window, as best he could with few teeth. 'We're looking for where they cremate fuckers! The cemetery.'

'Jesus!' It came out unheralded. The fact he just called my sister, his daughter, a *fucker*. 'No, not the cem—the Frederickson and Lane Funeral Parlour.'

The man at the bus stop moved over to my dad's window. I still couldn't see him properly to work out what he was wearing. He wasn't randomly colourful, like the African women you see on Electric Avenue on their way to church. His outfit was beige but—

'Frederick and Lean Parlour,' my dad shouted, mangling the name.

'He's not fucking deaf—' I whispered. 'And it's Frederick*son* and—'

The man was laughing, then talking.

'That's a nice shirt you got there,' to my dad. He sounded Caribbean. 'That for darts?'

'My daughter's funeral,' still shouting.

The man laughed deeply, then sombrely.

'I'm sorry for your loss, my man. Yeah, I know it. Yous runnin' late?'

'No we're not—' I checked the time; we were significantly early. But my dad interrupted.

'Probably.'

'I see, I see,' said the gent. 'I'll show you.'

And he opened the back door and got in. That's when I got a look at him, appearing to be dressed in full sheriff's outfit, badge on the shirt pocket, and a hat that was half ten gallon and half Rastafari. With chaps, a holster and gun on his, fair to say, big hips. A massive spliff behind the badge. The car suspension bunked backwards as he slammed the door.

Surely fancy dress, I said to myself. *Surely not a* real *gun.*

'Aye, I's knows, you drive on, sonny,' he said, and settled in the back seat, pulling my dad's crutches from the footwell so he didn't step on them.

I turned forward, both hands firmly on the wheel, 10 to 2, just like they teach you.

'On?' I asked. So tonal! 'Straight?'

'Yessir,' he said, waving me ahead. 'Yous keep headin' straight.'

I pulled into the road and got a quick glance at my dad. He had his gummy underbite jutting out in an ancient pose of satisfaction. I guess, funeral aside, this was probably the most entertaining day he'd had for twenty years. (Not counting his flings; trying not to think about the entertainment *they'd* provided.) And he'd been proven right: my Google maps *had* been useless, and we *had* found an old person to direct us. An old man with a *gun*.

In the rear-view mirror Sheriff was taking things in his stride, as if it was always his plan to requisition a member of the public's ride to get him to whatever crime he was on his way to investigate (or commit). (God, that sounded racist. I meant, because *gun*. With a gun! Maybe that's why he knew Frederickson and Lane Funeral Parlour, because he was da man who put da bodies—ridiculous. And what with the accent: racist, right? It was only plastic.)

'Wha' your names?' he asked from the back seat. His hands were resting over his belly.

'Roy,' my dad spittled, quite a feat without plosives. Then added, 'short for Royston.'

Sheriff laughed another deep belly laugh, and I wondered if he knew—and liked—the fact my dad was taking the piss. *Royston*. One, a Jamaican name.* Two, a bloody lie. My dad's name was not Roy or Royston. My dad put his wobbly right hand back over his shoulder for Sheriff to shake, and the man took my dad's hand in both his and shook them.

'And this is my son Ray,' my dad added. I quivered but not enough, I hoped, for Sheriff to see. Another lie, although a half one this time. Ray was my middle name.

'Roy and Ray,' said Sheriff, leaning forward as much as he could over his gun belt, chaps and belly. 'Tch, good Jamaican names,' laughing again. 'Lik da DJs in the 60s, Roy-1 and U-Roy, dub heroes. I'm Murvan. Nice to meet you. Sorry again for your loss.'

'Thanks Marvin.'

'Muar-van,' he repeated.

'Nice to meet you Marvan,' said my dad.

'Where next Murvan?' I asked, precisely vowelling, immediately feeling like a wanker for wanting to show up my unteachable dad. We were approaching a set of traffic lights.

'Straight over, Ray,' and he laughed again. I couldn't help but smile myself, now I was pretty sure it wasn't a real gun. In fact, it was a gift, this appearance. A third-party witness. Another opportunity for Capital-A Adult to show his quality.

'So where you headed?' I asked. 'To be fair, that's quite an outfit...'

'My uniform?' and from what I could see of him in the rear-view mirror, Murvan looked pleased. 'Gonna take care of some bisness.' Another laugh. Not mine this time. Oh god. But no, really? *Take care of...* 'I'll get out at the Funeral Parlour.' *See, he knows it! Why does he—* 'my bisness just round da corna.'

'Child's party?' I offered, struggling now, stretching for some clamp on reality. These days, didn't overdoting parents prefer to go for university students dressed up as Disney princesses, or choreographers to coordinate TikTok takeovers, or at the very least, clowns? Which parent in their right mind would hire a loaded Jamaican Sheriff for their kid's party?

'You running some gangsters outta town?' my dad asked, giggling.

'Aye, some hoodlums I bin aksed to rid the people of,' he said, both deadpan and magnanimous at the same time. 'Royston, tch, you know the ones, I see it, you bin cross their paths alriddy this day. Bad men. Turn right at the next turn, Ray,' Sheriff Murvan finished. And he laughed, and my dad laughed with him, and I would've laughed too if I wasn't thinking, *this is fucking weird, this is beyond* two cream doughnuts *weird, how the* fuck *did he know about* the Fash *earlier?* I shut up in time to remember he was talking to me, I was Ray, and turned right. Accessories. Would we be accessories? Were the bad men more Fash? We were into town proper now. Plenty of people about (plenty of older people at other bus stops not dressed in Wild West Indies regalia) and lines of shops, traffic, buses, a typical Monday lunchtime in a seaside pinkie-white town in England in the twenty-first century, except this figment of bizarreness really was happening, wasn't it? I was driving a Caribbean angel of death in sheriff's outfit to god knows what while the rest of my sister's mourners, her widower, my uncle, were standing in front of mirrors, quietly making Oxford knots in black ties, my aunt fussing with something in the kitchen to keep her hands busy, my sister's friends, Tracy, explaining to their husbands that there was no need for them to come, no, so the girls from Iceland and the Post Office could go and have a drink and smoke after. All were filling the minutes that could be filled with ways to evade thinking the thought of cremating a person that day, a person they loved. What is the quality of such time? Can you honestly think yourself inside the cremator, the flames and coffin, to the body, your loved one there, then not? And yet how could these minutes be filled with any other thought, how could you be distracted from thinking the central thought, unless the *distracting* thought was *so* overstrange, *so* outlandish, unfathomable... such *as,* for example, picking up a Jamaican Sheriff called Murvan and escorting him to do da bisness? So I wondered, again, if the universal field was showing its benevolence to my father—to me—to distract us from the double pain of grieving a death *and* the exertion of being in one another's company. What other reason could there be for him: Murvan the Manifest?

'Left now, son,' Murvan said. I turned left and we came into sight of the seafront. Murvan and my dad, Royston, *Royston!,* were conversing, and I realised I'd missed most of what they'd been talking about. Or rather, it'd been my dad talking, Murvan listening. And I knew then, surely, that it *was* the universal quantum field made apparent in this big Jamaican (again: racist; could be from another island. Why not St Lucia? St Kitts?) who had come in fancy dress to ease my dad's pain (and mine! don't be shy of the pain) like one big puff on a spliff. I knew there was no other reasonable explanation.

'And I don't know whyyyy...' my dad repeated, in the exact tone he'd said it to me twice before, having learnt nothing, rethought nothing, at the tail end of his sob-story about why his daughter disowned him. 'Didn't want me to see her off. But I'm coming anyway, looks like.'

And I don't know why! Christ.

Murvan let out a deep sigh.

'Saying goodbye to a child,' he shook his head slowly. 'Ah, left at that crossing, Ray.' He sighed again. 'Not far now. Not far. Roughest ting you can do. Saying goodbye to one who shoulda' outlive you, Royston. She was a beauty, ayes?'

She was obese and had crumbling teeth ruined by a childhood gorging on the emotional comforts of Marathon bars and Pepsi, I thought unkindly but not untruthfully. The weight she never unburdened herself of, that *he* loaded on her through a diet of trauma, most more than anyone. But what was the point of even thinking it, let alone saying it, to this stranger? (Except he wasn't a stranger, was he? Murvan was me, and I he, and both of us my father, all one with the universal field and its taking-the-piss-Creator.) I checked the rear-view mirror, caught Murvan's eyes on me. His whites were yellow, his pupils a deep dark brown. He didn't blink. I turned back to the road.

If he's heading to a child's party, I thought, *then I'm Marie Antoinette.* Which I supposed, at some coordinate on the infinite universal field, was actually the case.

'Now yous listen to mi words, Royston,' he said, and sat forward, picking up one of my dad's crutches to wring it with both hands in opposite directions, Chinese Burn style (and I thought, *now that's racist too, right?* Something I'd never considered before). 'You listen up. You too, Ray. Ray, pull up here, weis here, aye, look there's your place.'

Where? I looked at the row of stores on the far side of the road, beyond an expanse of promenade. We were, I noticed, by the pier. I squinted; I couldn't see a funeral parlour.

'Now, Royston.' He breathed in like he was deep diving for pearls, 'Royston, yous say goodbiy to ya daughta gud and tru, bruder, you hear mes? Yous no kip it in yous heart. Yous let it out. She hears yous, tru ting. And yous Ray,' and I jumped a little as I turned, and got one of those awful pings in my neck that causes you to realise that your vulnerable parts are made out of something a lot less durable than you'd always hoped, 'yous not let yous fadda outta yous sight, yous hear me? For once he's gin, he's gin.'

Then he laughed and it shook the car. My father laughed with him, and held his shaky hand out again to be grasped by Murvan's huge mitts. Why was I not laughing?

Murvan opened the car door.

'Off ta do ma bisness,' he said.

He pulled himself out. The car reared up. He slammed the back door and was off, strolling along the promenade. We watched him diminish—which took a while.

'Nice bloke,' said my dad.

I waited for a gentle magic to fall over me, and I waited, but it didn't come.

(*Royston, as it happens, is originally an English name. From the Yorkshire town of Royce; the name meaning Royce's Town, Royce being a derivation of royse, Old English for rose, and most famously retained in the fossil-fuel engine manufacturer moniker Rolls-Royce. But it is also a Jamaican name; and I pondered after, a long while after, how a Yorkshire appellation travelled to the Caribbean and back again, into the hands of my father as a joke.)

★

But now we were in a testing situation. As *nice bloke* as Murvan the Manifest may have been, he wasn't telling the truth about Frederickson and Lane. Along the row of shops across the road there was no funeral parlour to be seen. When I returned from searching, my father was out of the car on his crutches and looking at the sea beyond the pier. It was a grainy, muddy blancmange with the odd whip of eggwhite surf cresting and falling into the groyned frequencies of pebbled beach. He stood there for a moment and my heart formed a lump—this was probably the first time he'd seen the sea for maybe two, three decades. I couldn't go a month without the sea; a walk, a swim, something. And my lumpish heart was for him but also what was to come for me—for all of us, I supposed. The things we love that become unavailable to us as we age and immobilise. Family and the sea. Companions and chocolate. The projects we wanted to contribute to, the things we wanted to make. The world we wanted to immerse ourselves in. How completely over it all will be for us, one day.

But not completely. Compost for the worms. Molecules for the ocean. Cream for the doughnuts.

I stood next to my father and the breeze sent a waft of his stale jeans up my nose.

'There's no funeral parlour.'

'Nah, nahimbaemae,' he mumbled in a tone of... well, acceptance; of actually having listened to Murvan the Manifest. Leaving me in the difficult position of identifying this easy-come-easy-go attitude as the right one, but wishing he'd begun using it forty-eight years earlier and hadn't waited for a talking-to from a sheriff from ~~Jamaica~~ Anguilla. 'We early?'

'What's the time?' I asked.

'What, you don't have a watch?'

Ah, there you are! *Disappointment o'clock.* Back to normal.

'Only my Garmin, for running,' I explained. 'I just use the phone.' I looked around, hoping a town clockface on a side of the leisure centre or pier would help me out.

'No use that,' he said, and turned his wrist as well he could while leaning on the crutches. My father had always worn his watch face underneath, with the cloudy Citizen timepiece positioned where you would normally take a pulse. 'Eleven,' he said.

'We're early then.' Very, I didn't say. God knows how.

'Good,' he said, and started stalking. He shouted back. 'You said the pier has a bar?'

It did. And it was eleven, so it had probably opened. I thought, *well I can charge my phone there,* so I let him wander and went back and grabbed the phone from its cradle and the wires and hoped there was a USB port or that someone in the bar would have a charger.

It was as I remembered from the wedding reception. Decorated like one of those Estate Agent pictures on parody social media accounts, all black and chrome, Jack Vettriano paintings with waiters holding umbrellas over diners dancing on the beach. Although that sounded harsh: I'd liked it, to be honest, as a post-wedding venue— lots of exits and reasons to be outside. Pre-funeral? Maybe it lacked the velvet plushness of a windowless boozer that was necessary for softening some grief. Never mind, though, as my dad was already at the bar with two pints of Guinness halfway on the pour and settling heads before the top up. I joined him.

'Where do you want to sit?'

He looked around. He pointed with a crutch. 'There.'

A seat at the window, with a sea view. Where his daughter had sat, on her wedding day. As if that pesky universal field was up to its tricks again, and she was still there somehow, or her aura was, her molecules, the bridalgowned corona of a dead daughter.

'Go grab it then,' I said.

Other than the staff, we were the only people in the place.

He lurked off jerkily, reminding me of those beasties in *The Neverending Story**, the name escaped me (*it was *The Dark Crystal*, and the nasty beasties were the Skeksis) although not as tall, beaky, nor soulsuckingly evil. I went to pay, but he'd done so already. The barman topped up the drinks and I carried them over to our seats.

We sat opposite each other, my dad on the slidey vinyl bench with his back to the window and me opposite. I would have offered to swap, but he'd chosen it (right where my sister had sat) and the reorganisation (feet, crutches) wasn't worth it. Maybe the sea made him too sad. Maybe he didn't care for it. I wondered where his postings were, before the age of ten, with his mother and father in the army; if they were seaward. In Africa? The Mosquito Coast? Glasgow certainly wasn't coastal, and what I knew of the Clyde was industrial and rank, not a water for swimming or dreaming. And then he'd lived in Airdrie, anyway, moved to Bristol, and finally London. All rivered cities, but tumbling into poetic submersion was undoubtedly not a priority for a young Glasgee whip taking on engineering apprenticeships and proper jobs, and meeting my mum. The Cat's Whiskers. They were both only twenty. So young. Divorced by twenty-six. I couldn't even.

We drank a little of our cold Guinnesses in silence, and I only realised it was silence when one of the staff started up the music in the background, something from after 2006, which meant I didn't have a clue who it was. But something in the rhythm... maybe it was reggaetón (something H had introduced me to; oh H! No, hold on... it E with the reggaetón, I think) made me think of Murvan. Murvan the Manifest, like a guardian angel of the jest, soul brother to Thalia, goddess of comedy. Greek, sure, but no one said she was Caucasian!

'Who do you think he was?' I asked my dad.

He'd got Guinness in his moustache.

'Who?'

Who, F-F-S!

'Murvan.'

'Some loon.'

'A loon you invited into the car.'

'No I didn't.'

'Bu—' and actually, no, he hadn't, had he? Murvan had invited himself. His words to my dad flowed back to me. *Yous say goodbiy to ya daughta gud and tru. Yous no kip it in yous heart.*

'Did I.'

'No, fair enough, you didn't.' I'd had half the pint, breakfast a long time ago, and it was already affecting me, the Guinness, my hibitions becoming less in*ed* by the sip. Good. I had to get back in the car and drive, sure, but good, for now. Oh god, I'd forgotten about charging the phone. I looked under the table, under the bench he was sat on, but no plug with a USB port. So I'd just have the one drink. One was good. I'd ask the staff. For charging. But I wanted to know,

'You going to do what he told you? What Murvan told you?'

My father looked at me with that look. The one you give when you're trying to figure out how you can get *around* the pile of rubble and escape, not stop and hear the cries and dig out the person *underneath* the pile of rubble. (This may not be a *literal* situation people would have *actually* faced, but *metaphorically*, you understand (half a pint *in*ed!), metaphorically! And the person under the rubble? Your true Self, of course, your Soul, the rubble being... Ah, did I tend to overmetaphorise when drunk? Did I!)

Didn't matter anyway; he wasn't listening.

'I'll be missing my fruit,' he said, taking a swig. His Guinness was almost gone.

'Fruit?'

'On Mondays she gets me fruit when she does her shop.' He put the pint down with a slam. 'Vi, from No.30. Told you about her. I get her some when I go on Thursdays.' (Alongside the cream doughnuts; I pictured the laden trolley.) 'So it's always fresh.'

'No you didn't.'

'Didn't what?'

'Tell me about Vi.'

He shook his head, as if it was *my* memory that was faulty. *Nah, nahimbaemae!*

'What do you like?' I asked. 'We can get you some fruit.'

He shook his head. 'Not the same.'

No, of course bloody not. Not from me!

'Well don't bloody expect anything of nutritional value at the wake,' I said, still bitter about the wedding buffet. Then he giggled and told me the story of his friendship with Vi.

'Only decent fucker in that place,' which was not true, I knew, from his Christmas card efforts and the rolls of wrapping paper and gift bags he kept in the cupboard; knew from the floral stickers, the ones you get when you buy a pot of flowers, the bud and Latin name to prod down in the soil so you didn't forget what they were; he had a dozen of these stuck to his kitchen table legs. They'd obviously been gifts for some woman (women?) (men?), gifts anyway, which I'd confirmed by seeing the hundred and fifty quid he spent per month on flowers on a bank statement he'd left out on the kitchen table during a visit, something I'd noted with quizzicality when he'd popped off to the loo. They were definitely gifts. There were no living plants in his bedsit, although at the hothouse temperature he kept it at, it could have rivalled Kew.

Vi turned out to be happily married, a friend and comrade in arms (often quite literally: crutch support) in the sheltered housing where he'd been sandwiched between The Pits of Death; Vi was someone who survived (fruit! vitamins and minerals!) and now breathed the free air of south London four floors above with a view as far as the Croydon thrupney bit tower. They'd bonded when he first moved in and he'd needed help on a trip back to the hospital. He was weak then, having just emerged from the year on the ward recovering from his collapse, multiple heart attacks, the operations to remove many Skeksissy bits of his feet, and the COPD wracking his lungs. So Vi had gone with him. When the nurse asked for next of kin (I'd not reappear for another decade) he pointed to Vi.

'She's my sister,' he'd told the nurse.

He did have two real ones of his own, but they'd disowned him a long time ago, in response to his disowning them for their betrayal of staying with the family at the time of the Glasgow Jettison. (Being aged six and four, it was unlikely his sisters bore much responsibility for this. And yet, round and round we go on this wheel of life—and if you're like my dad, like a scratchy pointer that takes off the skin on every passing.)

The nurse had looked at them with an impatient tilt, tapping pen. They'd both giggled.

'Adopted,' Vi added, patting my dad's arm.

'She's Black, in't she,' he told me, finishing his Guinness. Giggling at the memory. 'My sister!' A full phlegmy laugh. 'Same colour as Marvin, actually. Caribbean.'

'Murvan. Caribbean a colour, is it?'

'Grapes, and strawberries. Blueberries. I can'ae eat all that citrus shite. Apples, too. Give me a bad belly. But berries'll do.'

'We can—' I began, but I'd already offered. It wasn't fruit, but, 'another pint?'

'Aye, one last one,' he said, squinting at me.

'You've not answered my question.'
'What question?' he laughed, as if he already knew.
'You going to do what he told you?' I asked again. 'Murvan?'
'My memory is fucking appalling,' as an excuse.
'You've forgotten what he said?'
My dad licked his lips and removed the soapy bits of Guinness from his moustache.
'Remind me.'
Diving for pearls! With a knife between the teeth. Deep breath.
'Yous say goodbiy to ya daughta gud and tru, bruder, you hear mes? Yous let it out.'
In my best (worst) Jamaican accent. I surprised myself, and saw I'd surprised him too. He didn't laugh; worse. I'd caught him off guard. Every ounce of joy from telling the story of Vi dropped from his face. Every reminder of death crowded his brow.
'Oh, I'm—' but he shook his head and waved me to stop.
He sat for a moment with a beaten glower, his chops sucked into his cheeks where his teeth should have been. He was an old man, a child inside still, but old, old. I'd thought he was old when he picked me up on the 6.30am mornings to drive us to work at the engineering factory those summers of my teens, so I could earn a few pounds and be in his orbit; thought he was old when I saw him off the booze for the first time in his life, withered and skinny, at my stepmom's 60th, the last time I saw him before he disappeared; but no. *Now* he was old. Before, he'd been *getting older*. Now *I* was the one getting older. He'd passed the point when that would happen. He was not on the journey any longer. He'd reached the destination. He'd always be old now. And not healthy enough to get to very. Never reaching very.
'I know I wasn't—' he began. His hand involuntary reached for the Guinness glass but it was empty. He looked at me as if something he'd scribbled in the margins of a word puzzle had come back to him. As if a hidden word in that puzzle—maybe *fatherly*; maybe *touched*—had caught him off guard, hit him unexpectedly, and made him think—no, realise—no, *feel*—that now he had a son again. A

son who'd looked for him, turned up, came and took him for his first drink in a decade, and was driving him to this funeral. What did he want to say to a son like that? I waited. Was it coming? Would it ever come? He looked like he'd lost the thread. How long was I going to wait?

'When you turned up,' he began. Then shook his head. 'At my door. Jesus Christ.'

Ahoy! Impatience. I blinked half a dozen times and waited for him to carry on. Should I prompt him? I'd been waiting a bloody long time, could I wait any longer?

'What about your daughter?' I said in the end.

He looked like I'd hit him. Not only because I'd reminded him of the child who had disowned him; but also simultaneously deflected him off the trail of that word puzzle thought, that memory of wanting to connect: of what he'd wanted to say to *me*. About *us*.

'What about you, *Ray*?' he asked, and giggled. And there he went again! I'd inadvertently rerouted his mind back to that place the drink took him. Into the Panic Room of his Inebriated Soul where he did not have to explain things, nor feel his way through the labyrinthine word puzzle of life. The ruts in his mind so worn down there was no other track for the thoughts to travel. As soon as they arose, the wheels rode right back into the potholes, especially if the fucker on the other side of the pub table provided a push.

There were times the wheels hadn't... that time he was sober for a year before my stepmother's 60th. It was during that time that *he* wrote to *his* father and reconciled the relationship with The Glasgow Jettisoner, as his father, my grandfather, lay dying in the Chelsea Hospital (the *Royal* Chelsea Hospital... graveyard for institutionalised veterans who couldn't re-enter civilian life). But my father's mind was mush by then (his father's too). And all he did at my stepmother's 60th birthday party was stand in the lounge by his fish tank and look mournfully at the rest of us and cry. His mind didn't know how to work without the booze and fags. The ruts were too deep, the troughs didn't crumble. He was forlorn, pitiable, a skinny human on the lam from all he'd done. Terrible, but

I preferred him as the bastard: safe in his Panic Room, not conscious of the depth of his own pain as he had been when sober. Rather stuck in the rut than falling through the cracks.

'Wha?' I asked, Caribbean again, rising intonation. As light-hearted as possible. But it was too late for that. He didn't play along.

'Not gonna let me out of your fucking sight are you, in case I make a problem with her bloody husband's *differences*? That's what he said, Marvin?'

Oh, memory okay now then, daddio?

'Something like that.' Break the surface for breath! 'It's Murvan. Shall I get the drinks?'

'I need a piss,' he said. I reached for his crutches. 'Nah, nahimbaemae,' he muttered and snatched them from me and stood up. He menaced his way through the empty seats to the bathroom, camouflaged in his black and silver darts top against the chromatic décor of the pier bar. He came into focus against the fluorescent light that shone through the open toilet door, and with a push of his crutches, he disappeared inside.

And I thought, *well, sorry Murvan, failed you already*.

*

I ordered two more Guinnesses and asked if anyone had a phone charger. No one could help. The Eagles' *Lying Eyes* came on the bar's stereo and I took the drinks back to our seats and sat down. I never knew I could do a Caribbean accent. All those episodes of *Desmond's* had come in useful. A terrible generalisation, and I flagellated by becoming serious and speculating. Just how many different accents and languages there were across the islands? But not a *colour*. At least not a colour! To be fair, I thought we'd got away with Murvan's ridealong without an awful clanger. But now I was left wondering, *what the hell*... no Frederickson and Lane Funeral Parlour. No closer to the crematorium. He'd disappeared as quickly as he'd arrived. Could I remember him turning a corner? I believed in angels, in fact. (Long before the Ayahuasca.) I'd grown up with Catholicism and books about John Dee's conversations with angels in Enochian, but I *really* started believing that time I took a friend to the Byron Exhibition at the National Portrait Gallery. It was a symbolic setting, chosen as backdrop to give my friend a talking-to. He'd started a new relationship (with the charming T) and was at risk of ruining it with his drunken jealousy; his insecurity, of course, and I understood *that* like no other in our friendship group. So I happily pulled the short straw, and arranged to meet him at the gallery. We wandered through portraits of Byron the poetic knave and as we ambled, I passed on my advice of judicious balance: see T and his mates, but *don't* drink; see T and drink, but *no* mates; see his mates and drink, but *no* T. Just uncomplicate things for a while, until the tricky stage had passed. Until he could rebuild—more likely, build from scratch—the trust he needed to both feel and feel he could offer. Trust wasn't being given much air in the twenty-something's engine room of cramming as many social events, drinks, and arguments as possible into one weekend.

After the exhibition we went to the gallery's café and bought hot chocolates (wait! a *fourth* possibility? see his mates and *no* T and *don't* drink?!) and then wandered through Chinatown in the general direction of the underground. My friend was thankful but morose; he didn't know if he could build things slowly, or accept himself to be less than he imagined, in terms of his capacity for love (a lack of conviction that, alas, again, I knew too well). He finished his chocolato in haste and said goodbye. I was stood on the corner of Chinatown and Shaftsbury Ave worrying if I'd done the right thing to volunteer advice. I offered it from a place of compassion but not experience (if only someone—*like a dad?!*—had taken *me* aside, and given *me* advice on *my* relationships, perhaps I wouldn't be sitting alone in the pier bar staring at the cold blue sea).

So, I'd stood on Shaftsbury Ave, watching my friend wander away, shoulders sagging, wondering if I was in the right place after all. Which was when I got a tap on the shoulder, and a young Asian man wearing a baseball cap with the word ANGEL embroidered on it, asked me for directions. I knew where he wanted to go so

I turned in that direction, and saw in front of me, exactly where my finger was pointing, a plaque bearing the street number 44. The number 44, I should have explained, being a magical number, powerful in numerology (look it up!), a number which turns up at exactly those moments when I am lost and asking for direction in life, a little like when this young ma—but he'd disappeared. Fffppt. Gone, not even bothering with the fiction of directions. ANGEL on his cap. Pointing *me* to the 44 I hadn't, wouldn't have, seen without his guardianship. *Hark!*

So perhaps it *was* the best advice I've ever given anyone, to my friend, judged on its outcomes (he and his partner remain happily married with two wonderful kids, and for whom, I am, in fact, the favourite 'uncle' because of how I treat animals... but I vegress).

So: Murvan the Manifest. Another angel. What other explanation was there?

(Vegress = a vegan digress; supremely performative. To say it, does it.)

I'd been staring at the sea all this time. Half my Guinness was gone, and my dad still hadn't come back. If I went into the toilet and he was, I don't know, having an impacted shit or something and shoving a suppository up his bum, it would be too terrible, way beyond the tonal scourge of his *Nah nahimbaemae*, to rectify by simply backing out of the stalls and pretending I hadn't heard him. I waited a while longer. The bar was filled with more country music, maybe Dolly, maybe some other singer. I was nearly done with Pint Two and conjectured I might need a Pint Three to keep my dad company, but I also had to drive to the crematorium. So, no. I shouldn't even finish Pint Two.

A few early drinkers had drifted into the bar. The fear of coming upon my dad in wailing constipation kept me from going *in there*, and I felt more desperate for that last few mouthfuls of Guinness than I'd perhaps ever felt for a drink in my life, so to stop myself I got up and wandered outside as if going for a cigarette. I found myself looking down on the sea from the pier railing, the wind catching the surf. It was chill around the ears and I pulled up my collar to insulate the New Thought just come to mind, the New Thought being, of course, now I wasn't distracting myself: if Murvan *was* another ANGEL, then why had he turned up to direct us to the pier on the pretence that it was the location of Frederickson and Lane? And how had he known what to say... angels always know, of course, but... but... I was being ridiculous, wasn't I? Was I? When my grandfather (my mother's father, not the Glasgow Jettisoner) had died, I'd seen owls everywhere for weeks. They told me—who? YouTubers?—that grief can manifest in esoteric ways as well as the obvious. It materialises as a symbol of the person we don't want to let go, energies of their molecules intertwining with the undestroyed universal field. So grandfather = wise old bird. That made sense. Much more so than non-spiritus barn owls in suburban Bromley. But where was my dad? I couldn't shift the image of him with a suppository halfway into his rectum and it caused me great refusal, *great* refusal, to go looking for him or his pokey-headed turtle on a string; refusal to re-enter the bar, even. So I found myself strolling along the pier towards a black marquee being lightly whipped by the wind, a marquee with a blurry glowing sign out front. As I got closer, I could see the sign was made of sulphurous oversized lightbulbs like you find outside bougee cinema halls. I squinted and focused until it became readable: ALARM CLOCK it shone. A panel of the marquee was hooked back offering an entrance, but where to? What to? The insides were so black it was impossible to see what was entranced. A marquee! Incongruous and abandoned, here on the pier in a small seaside town, an impression extra charged by the fact no one was around. No attendant or ticket seller. Had my father come out of the toilet and fancied a cigarette of his own while I wasn't spying, seen the sign and also been intrigued? Was he inside *there*? Better that than what might be inside *him*! Anyway, if he was, more probably, now out of the loo and back at our seats he had a pint to drink, it's not as if he could run away. So *okay*, I thought, *what to? What to?!*

I poked my nose inside the marquee, feeling childish and threatened. It was almost pitch black. I tinystepped my way along, hands out to the side touching nothing but black space, and suddenly I felt the thrill of it: like a ghost train or house of mirrors. Its incongruity fell away; where *else* would a postmodern take on the frightener fairground attraction be situated, other than an old pier? My senses became sharper; I could smell cotton cloth, hear the faint swash of the sea. I had a sudden vertiginous experience of knowing that I was walking over water, separated only by clacking boardwalk, floating in a space of something darker than I knew. My eyes were adjusting, but it was my outstretched hand that found a heavy fabric veil that ran, with a little tugging, on a rail. The curtain shifted aside to reveal a purple-black door. I fumbled and turned the handle. The door opened inwards and I was hugged by warmer air. It felt inviting after the chill on the pier, so I went in. The door swung closed behind me, and I thought I heard or at least imagined the veil close with it.

This room was less black. I could make out shapes, although not what the shapes were. The warmth, now I was inside, was a little stifling. My eyes adjusted and I saw myriad large paintings or perhaps photographs around the walls, scenes I could make out as I came closer: dinghies crowded with small faces and bodies in lifejackets; a huge combine-harvester-like machine in a forest, mowing down trees; a helicopter dropping a huge white parcel; a single rhino and six armed guards; a long queue of people snaking around a car park waiting to enter another marquee, also black. I noticed a glow above my head and looked up. There was a digital clock with a very dim display showing 20:33. It was faintly blinking. I stood and watched for a second; in fact, at least sixty-one, as I counted the blinking colon between the digits. It did not roll around to 20:34 but sat on 20:33. Of course, that wasn't the time anyway. So what was it? I looked around. There were three gaps in the portraits: a black space with a glint of steel, the door I came through; and then two other faint signs in dulled neon, not readable until I got closer. One said *Exit*, the other *Off Ramp*. I pondered what *Off Ramp* might mean but got the fear and it wrung the neck of my curiosity and I left it for the brave. I inched towards the *Exit* and pushed open the door.

Jesus Christ! Opened onto nothing, mid-air, a fucking drop into the sea! Unrailed edge of the pier! No bastard barrier! Wind galed and threshed me back and forth and I grabbed the sides to stop myself tumbling eighty foot into the English Channel. The sides I'd grabbed were curtain with considerable give and I tilted out thirty degrees staring into the water like a wide-eyed and less buxom Kate Winslet on the Titanic. The curtains held, and I heaved myself backwards. Out of the way, the hinges automatically swung back to close. I was ensconced again in muffle, blackness, sea spray and sweat. Had I fallen over? I was sitting, so I had. But my god. Where was Leo when you needed him? Where was passenger third class Jack Dawson to clasp me by the waist and sing Celine Dion into my ear?

Fucking hell.

I stood up, fuzzy legged and wonky.

Then: had my *dad* taken the *Exit*?

He wouldn't have got this far, with crutches. Too bloody cynical to step foot in. Silly idea. No. I took a few deep breaths. Calmed myself.

Okay. *Off Ramp* it was then.

But a different thought. I went back the way I'd come in. But there was no handle this side of that door. The glint of metal I'd seen was in fact a little plaque, with an almost impossible to read inscription. I hunched down to make it out.

Told you so.

Had they? Who? When?!

There was no way to open the door so I turned to the *Off Ramp*. Spatially it was 90 degrees to the *Exit*, so couldn't be, I hoped, another watery death trap. (A death trap by other means? Surely possible.) I crept over very slowly. I kneeled, in fact, as I pushed open the door. Other than an obvious increase in temperature, a stinking stale air filling my nostrils, it seemed a similar room, dim enough to catch edges of images around the wall and another digital clock hanging from the ceiling. I went in. The door slipped close behind.

God, the heat. The cold sweat was swatted away, my arms and

back became immediately prickly. I scanned, letting my eyes accustom. Objects in the room, looming, sinister, again I wasn't sure what they were. I looked for the *Exit* and *Off Ramp*, could see two blurry small signs, barely glowing in the shadows. I put a hand behind me to feel over the surface of the door I'd come through to discover if there was another plaque: there was. I brought my eyes close and squinted at the inscription.

Wakey, wakey!

I was meant to feel... attacked? entombed? I guess, probably yes. But who put this bloody thing here? And fuck, Jesus Christ, that *Exit*? Health and safety?! Was that the point? In the centre, hanging from the ceiling, another digital alarm clock. This one blinking 20:43, a ten-digit advance. I stepped slowly around the walls again, fearing false floorboards, avoiding the black shapes, concentrating to parse the images: a kangaroo amidst the ruins of a wildfire; an industrial port from above, a thousand shipping containers toppled over like dominoes; an abandoned street, shops boarded up; a hundred people clinging onto the wheels of a plane as it takes off; a blown-up image of a virus; a shed full of dead pigs.

The first door I came to said *Off Ramp* again, but this time the second said not *Exit* but *No Exit*. I pushed it open slowly. Another room, but even through that small gap I felt its terrible heat pressing on my face. I crept back to the *Off Ramp* door, and pressed it open ever so gently. Another room: lighter, and cooler. Okay. Okay. I stepped in but not gently enough to avoid faltering, the sensation when you put your foot out into empty air. I stumbled forward, my shoes submerged in water right up past my ankles. To the shinbones and beyond! Fuck! Soaking wet feet. And my good wedding-funeral shoes, too.

I had a funny feeling in my gut, like the Guinness curdling. It was lighter in here. There was the alarm clock: 20:43. Same as the room I'd just come from. Hmm. No other doors though. I looked around. There were a few extra images. Were they worth the slosh? Water had splashed its way up to my knees. I decided against it. Soggy legged, I exeunted into the hotter, darker room, made my way over to the *No Exit*, and slowly went through.

Jesus, the heat. It was intolerable. I wasn't sure I could breathe. I bent over, the air less burn-the-lungs around the knees. It was pitch black, and for the first time I felt properly scared. Not shocked by almost falling into the sea. Not ghost train frighted. Scared I had potentially lost my mind. Scared that this wasn't real at all, scared that I'd somehow fallen into a cavern in my cognizance and couldn't, wouldn't, get out. That I'd dissociated from reality. I touched both elbows with opposite hands to check I was real. I checked my waterlogged legs. Still wet. I lifted my head to look for signs but couldn't see anything. Shit. What if I was trapped here? What if there was no way out?

Then the flashes started. A beat, a pulse of red light lit the room. In that moment I caught a glimpse of the pictures on the walls, or rather, the pictures being the walls. One wall was trees on fire. Another a flood torrent washing cars down a street. Another a hurricane tearing a roof off a house, palm trees bent sideways. The fourth a pile of what looked like elephants, skinned, their red-white muscle and bone exposed to the sky. Amidships in the polydisaster, the intersecting shitshow. I looked up: there was the alarm clock. Glowing 20:53.

I dropped to my knees, waited for the next pulse. I was soaked in sweat. The pulse came. I scanned for a door. Pitch, breathe, pulse, scan. Nothing. Shit! Pulse. It was then I noticed a sound with the pulsing light, a sonic beat like a very slow heart. Pulse. Okay, be systematic. One wall at a time. Doors likely in the middle. Pulse. The trees on fire. Couldn't see. Pulse. Flood, no. Pulse, hurricane, what was that? The house having its roof ripped off had a door, and it looked like it had a handle. I crawled towards it. Yes! A handle, and a sign. I stood up. Fuck, the heat! My oesophagus desiccated a percent. I grabbed the handle and pulled down. It didn't open. Shit! I dropped to my haunches, tried the door handle from below. No. I took a breath and stood so I could read the sign. Waited for the pulse. The burst of red, and I read: not *Exit* but *Exist*.

What the actual.

I lay down. I curled up to catch my breath. *This isn't what I set out for this morning*, I thought, knowing how desperate it sounded, how doleful. *I didn't ask for this. I didn't deserve this. Jesus, I'm one of the good guys! I'm doing my bit!* But I got it nevertheless, of course I got it. Pulse. *I get it, okay! Now let me out.*

No *Exit*. Only *Exist*. Right.

Falling back, I must have pushed the door; it opened a crack. Blimey. All I had to do was push. I pushed again. It opened. Pitch black, but who cared. I crawled through, the door whacking my body as I caterpillared out. The heat was worse. But the pulses stopped. I crawled. But wait, which direction? I didn't have to worry, attempts to turn left or right batted me into a wall. I was in a corridor no wider than the door's width. Jesus, I really had lost my mind. This would be the nightmarish scenario a film director would imagine what it must be to be psychotic. Locked in and unable to reverse out. It was like an episode of *Black Mirror*, or a *Saw* film, which I never could watch. Was I *being* filmed? *I'm A Bad Son Get Me Out of Here*? Was this a Derren Brown set up? Had I been hypnotised? Rather that, than the alternative. I'd sign that waiver in a heartbeat. I realised I hadn't called for help. I hadn't shouted. I wondered why. Maybe I already knew why. Anyway, it was too hot to cry out. I was wasting oxygen even thinking about it.

I crawled. Sweating enough to make it a slither. What a mess I was making of my suit. Propelling myself forward on my elbows and knees. It was difficult to look ahead, hard on the neck to rear up, and when I did there was nothing to see. Until there was, glowing at the end of the corridor. An exit? But what to?! As I crawled closer it came into focus. Four digits a colon, another alarm clock. I crawled, stopping to breathe. It was like being cooked in a pizza oven. A last drag. The alarm clock came into view.

20:63.

Not minutes then. But I knew that anyway.

But so what? We *had* years, didn't we? I was doing something, wasn't I? This was just an exhibit, some sort of immersive theatre, wasn't it? I *was* doing something about the crisis! I would do more if

I could just get out of this corridor, this heat, I'd do more. *I would!* I even congratulated myself for having already been involved. *Congratulated myself!* For taking it all seriously. I didn't need this warning. I was warned! I knew the crisis was coming. I partook in the resistance! Partook! Oh, what a prize wanker the ego is. The *I* is. Soaking, wailing, crawling. Oh yes, well done. *Well done!* Idiot. And bitterness then, a cry of a child. *This marquee was not meant for me*, I cried! *Not for me!*

But then I was the one crawling out of it, so maybe it was.

I slunk on, instincts kicked in. Closer to the alarm clock my elbows started to bump the walls. My head bumped the ceiling of the corridor. It was getting *lower*? Of course it was getting lower! Down to the smallest possible gap as all other options became untenable, inescapable. I closed in on the alarm clock, my breath taken from me through the claustrophobia, the heat, the fear, and then not even the fear, just grief, just misery, for the why of it, the why, why we were being forced to crawl this corridor on our bellies, unaccepting and afraid. Everyone (except the billionaires). And for what? What to? Some already were crawling. Already burning to breathe. So many already dying. I cried my pitiful tears and they hissed on my cheeks. I crawled on. I passed under the alarm clock and for a moment got stuck, no more width to wriggle through. I cried, I cried. The polydisaster! The shitshow! What a wanker I was, crying. But I cried for the animals, didn't I? The trees. Not for my*self*?

Yes, *and* for myself. Right at that moment, to be truthful, only for myself.

My head butted a wall. It opened a crack and in gusted cold air and daylight. I pushed with the top of my balded head and I could see the thick old boards of the pier just beyond, the sea below. It was freezing and for a moment, the shortest flash, I thought, wouldn't it be more comfortable in the oven? Wouldn't it be okay to just fizzle out?

But the part of me that wanted life pushed on. I'd escape. I wriggled onto the pier. It was a hatch just big enough for me. Out of the blue it made me think of the cat flap I used to crawl through as a kid, when I'd come home from school but had forgotten my key. It wasn't a snazzy plastic cat flap; my stepfather, mum's second husband, had been a spendthrift and had sawn a hole out of the back door, put hinges on it and a bolt, added to lock the neighbourhood Toms out. Our cat Sylvester had been a big lad, you could say, bless his tuxedoed toes. Anyway, it was big enough for me when I was ten. Big enough for svelte burglars I imagined, but we never had any trouble (except with the Jehovah's Witnesses, and they wangled their way in through the front).

Then I was out. I would have lain there on the boards but I was suddenly freezing so I pulled myself up. The hatch I'd come through had closed. I peered down but could see no join. (My mum complained about the cold air getting in through the gaps in the cat flap. She would have welcomed the craftsmanship, nay, wizardry, on *this* hatch, sealing automatically. They divorced, my mum and Husband Number Two; she changed the locks on him, and he was neither as cunning as the JW to get in via the front, nor as narrow as Sylvester to crawl through the flap-back.)

I stood. The marquee also stood, like there was nothing strange to it at all. The sign still shone out ALARM CLOCK but the entrance had closed. I rubbed my face vigorously. I opened my eyes. I looked around. Nothing else had changed. The sea was still cold, crashing, cresting. I took in the rest of the pier. Without another thought I walked back to the bar.

The doors were shut. I rattled them. Locked.

I peered inside. Chairs were stacked on tables. A sheet thrown over the bar. The remnants of a sticky sign that had been plastered on the door and either torn or weathered off. The bar looked as if it hadn't been open for some time. As in, months. Maybe years.

Oh hell, I thought. Oh hell.

I stumbled back to the car in the daze of a disaster survivor. My suit certainly was—a disaster. Crumpled, sweaty. The car was where I'd left it, and easy to spot, as there weren't many others about. There were people strolling along the seafront, in and out of the cafés and shops on the far side of the road. A long, single-deck bus drove past, full of people. I went to pull my phone out of my pocket to check the time, but it wasn't there. Had I left it in the bar? On the table? But the bar wasn't open. Hadn't been. And where was—

I still had my car key and got in, put hands on the wheel. I started up the engine, heard the rattle of the exhaust pipe, felt, as I pulled out, the drag of the slow puncture in the rear passenger side wheel, pulling the car to the left. I was driving. But where was I going? Where to?! I drove slowly, heading to the only place in town I knew—my sister's. Past the Aldi, which I was relieved to see was doing business, although the car park was mostly empty. I had the urge to stop and think for a bit. What was with the no cars? *Told you so.* Who? And hadn't I just aband—. Surely it wasn't the bar *we'd* been in but another part of the show, a sham, a replica of the real bar on the other side of the pier? Or something? *Or something!*

But there was no other side. I drove on. Through town. Turned and followed the quiet, twisting roads through a housing estate, more of a bungalow estate, really. When Kels and Gavin had bought No.15, they lowered the average age by quite a slice, and had to reassure all their fellow bungalowers that, no, they didn't like to party.

I turned into their cul-de-sac. I pulled up. Things looked familiar. The next-door neighbour's classic motorbikes were out on his driveway and blocking the path to his front door, a fact his wife, I'd been told, never stopped complaining about. One was a beautiful old Triumph Trident, a radical three-cylinder, gold and chrome and expertly made, as if the engineer had been given all the time in the world to figure out how parts of a bike would ideally go together. Out of the blue, a memory came to me of my dad's handwritten CV: the engineering jobs I never knew he'd had before I was born, tool machinist and planer; the O-Levels he'd studied for at Coatbridge College, maths and engineering and drawing. It had broken me seeing that CV left on his kitchen table thirty years after it had been handwritten in pencil on lined paper, all caps; broken me that I had not been there when he'd needed a son with a computer, when he'd been a working man with something still to offer, but had no one to type it up and print it out. No son to help him with the job hunt, or the later journey into *older*, and then passed into the end-times, when a CV was no longer necessary. Maybe he hadn't known what Google was, after all... And where *was*—

—and there *she* was. My sister.

Coming out of the front door of her bungalow and trotting along the paved path and waving her vape at me. Perfectly alive and uncaramelized.

Oh hell.

I got it wrong, didn't I?

You already said that.

Oh, shut up.

I stretched and ran my hands over my head and face as if I'd just got out of bed and was still half-asleep. Which I hoped I was.

'Hello!' my sister said through the window in her always astonished, cheery voice, that made you think you were always interrupting a previous panic about something. She was alive. Strangely, that didn't make it any easier to look at her when she talked, for her rotten teeth from all those years of smoking, sugaring, Pepsi-ing, were not a nice sight.

I opened the window. 'Hello.'

She approached to say 'I'll just be a minute,' and seemingly without even stopping she turned and walked off and then stopped a moment, breathed deeply, and turned and came to the window and leant down. I could smell vape and bad teeth.

'What?' I asked as an opportunity to turn away.

'Gavin can't come.' I could tell straight away it was the birth of a lie. 'His manager's called in sick and he's the only one who can do today's deliveries from the warehouse.'

'Oh, okay,' I said, the words *bastard don't bring him here* rang in my ears and thinking, rethinking, *What, okay, I got it wrong, didn't I?*

My sister trundled off. She wasn't dressed for a funeral. Not yet, anyway. And certainly not her own. No. Not her own. Because, in fact. Because—

Part 2

GETTING HER TO THE FUNERAL presented a number of challenges.
One: I had fairly recent and compelling evidence to believe I was psychotic.
Two: No phone, so no map.
(Stop! Stop shaking your head at me.)
Three: Where the hell was I going, anyway? Which funeral?!
Four: (returning to the birth of the lie only ten seconds in) I had during life tolerated my father's weakness for making things up better (can you believe it?) than my sister's dishonesties. There was good reason for this. First, there were lies of hers that she had told about *me*; being siblings, I had right of rebuttal. Power decreases tolerance, I've found. Only the powerless must endure; and powerless is the status of the child whose parents lie. So I endured my father's lies (patriarchal, Moses-like, unassailable) but my sister's lies did not have to be tolerated. For example, Exhibit A: when I received my G.C.S.E. results (of *'Shoulda' called you Judas'* infamy) she'd said I came home bragging *shoving them up my nose*. (*Under*, I corrected her.) I had not. Yet she retold this fib to our maternal granddad, whose time and solidity she dominated. My grandad turned against me. So: challenge her lies, I did. My sister's false fancies were not unassailable. They were assailable *tout court*! I confronted her; a screaming match ensued. Of course, psychotic as I may have been sitting in the car outside No.15 (nicknamed Bleak House by my uncle and aunt), after having crawled through an overheating and collapsing time warp... as a *sixteen*-year-old, I most certainly had *not* been psychotic; in fact, I was *hyper*conscious of my behaviour. I was certain that I'd hidden the G.C.S.E. exam results for weeks, swallowing the shame of what my father had accused

me of—unbeknownst betrayal—the way it stuck in my throat like a piece of silver. *I had not bragged.*

But then certainty is relative if we take account of the universal field. And of how much we know of the way memory works, overwritten each time a story is retold.

Had I come home bragging?

No. We have to hold to some truths, don't we?

(BTW: I had more G.C.S.E.s (10) than A.C.E.s (6), in case the question comes up in the quiz. Oh, you didn't realise there was a quiz at the end? Get ready to *Let's Get Quizzical!*)

So, to sum up point four, I'd not managed to forgive my sister in the way I had (almost) my dad.

Five: could I get through a three-hour car journey with my sister? Without asking her why she lied? Was still telling the big lie to friends, such as Tracy, she of the healthy feet but unhealthy marriage, *Like?* I asked, *Like your dad breaking every bone in her body.*

Six, toughest: as already discussed, the relationship between my sister and father ended, for all intents and purposes (much blah blah, no blah blah) thirty-five years ago. No contact blah blah. And no. *NO.* It wasn't going to start up anytime soon, was it?

Seven: my sister didn't drink at all, which was almost as bad as my dad's alcoholism.

Eight: she smelled bad too. She had no excuse either. She was married and had a job.

Nine (related to *Four*): A memory of my father came to me, related to Kels's husband Gavin. The fact my dad had not wanted him *Don't bring that bastard* at any future funeral of his. Quid pro quo for the fact he wasn't invited to their wedding? I assumed so; the bitter, vindictive lot of 'em. I'd known my sister *she doesn't want him here* didn't want him at the ceremony, but hadn't realised how much Gavin didn't either, much to do with (it became clear, as I sat in the car waiting for Lady Dedlock to get dressed so we could leave for god knows where) because Gavin's dad hadn't been at their wedding. Anyway, a wedding is their day, the bride and groom's, and if my sister didn't want to *couldn't face it* my aunt told me, the past *inner work* was past (said my uncle) and she wasn't psychically prepared as *you are* (only just) to make the effort to *endure* each other's company—then so be it! I wondered, then, if my sister inviting me to give her away at her wedding instead of our dad was actually her way of making sure *I'd* turn up?

Ten: the bloody can opener had been well and truly twisted and turned, hadn't it?

I sighed, wishing for a brief moment that I was someone else. Pootering off on a shiny chrome and green Triumph Trident, perhaps, to some blessedly uncomplicated weekly gathering with pals from the Triumph Motorcycle Owner's Club down on the seafront, for a hot chocolate with marshmallows (not even bloody vegan! a different person!). Strictly three topics of conversation at this parallel life meet up: 1) Triumphs; 2) other brands of classic British motorcycles; and 3) petrochemical-based sports (especially the sidecars, superbikes, and TT, but preferably not that jumped-up procession for Monaco-based show-offs, the F1).

Was any of this starting to make sense now?

I put my mind to it. What *were* encounters with The Fash, the Badger Liberation Army, Murvan, ALARM CLOCK: Marquee of Planetary Heat Death, and a car drive with a disappeared dad, trying to tell me? If not about psychosis, then what? I could only propose it was this universe's best attempts to support my cognitive dissonance and vain distraction to divert me from the task at hand: getting him, her—all of us!—to the funeral.

Which was where?

I really couldn't tell.

The door to Bleak House opened, its spirits (Gavin in his dressing gown, hot footing it to the warehouse, obvs) waving my sister off, and there she was, clunkily lowering herself into the passenger seat, and I was turning the car around to, yes, get her—get *us*—to, to—

A *funeral,* of course.

But where? Whose?

'Right then,' she said, a quick reassuring puff off her vape. She'd changed the flavour.

'Right then,' I agreed.
Only three hours in the car! No idea where I was heading! Nothing to fear!

*

Driving off this little promontory of eastern England was easier than navigating through a Monday London. One road out, basically. There were still disconcertingly few cars, and more of those long buses that I was sure I hadn't seen before. Anyway, one road for quite a long stretch, which was good, as I really wasn't sure… I had my suspicions, something was coming back to me through the hot haze of the black marquee, the thing that… had it, though? Had it? I took a glance at my feet in the pedal well, pressed on the accelerator and ready for the clutch. Were they wet? Could I feel squelchy toes? I couldn't tell. Anyway, they would have dried by now. So, for the sake of my sanity, I made a decision: yes, all of it *had* happened. *Was* happening. She'd come out of Bleak House in a black trouser suit with a white blouse and a grey overcoat. We were both dressed for a funeral.

Just not hers.

We did smallest talk for a few miles. How was the Post Office? Fine. How was my job, what was it I did again? Wrote stuff. Bit of tutorialising. It was fine. Gavin? Fine, oh you know, he's got his comics on eBay, buy-buy, sell-sell, he's planning to donate the collection to the comics museum (in return for a plaque bearing his name), his work was fine, lost weight too now he's walking to town (since they sold the car my aunt had bought them—and kept the money, btw; rip *that* lid off!). I wanted to ask about the lack of cars on the roads, but it wasn't the moment. Instead, there grew a silence where my sister would have asked about my partner if I had one, H or E or… But no, no question. My sister did the reciprocity of conversation well enough. Seen as a game of tennis: you lob one at her, she'd lob it back. The problem came when either you didn't lob, or the lob back was a booby, like this one: *but you don't have a partner to ask after*. So she was stumped (different sport, I know). She didn't *serve*, my sis. The hush stretched out past the next junction. About as comfortable as new jeans a distant cousin might buy you for Christmas. She struggled for the backhand, finally to ask,

'How's your pussy cat then?'

'Fine!' I replied. Note that *then*. Oh, the condescension! The feline replacement for human love! I could almost hear her thinking: *H got away, but the cat doesn't have a bloody cat flap!* (She does. I've tried shoving her through it. Tried it myself, for old times' sake. But she's too aloof for such degrading exits, my princess-Misha-monkey-moochy-mooch-mooch.)

Avoiding looking my sister's way, I turned forward, a clear road ahead. I studied the dashboard, and saw that I was below half a tank of fuel. Okay. My head was still a bit woozy from… well, from all of it. A bar of something, some protein snackage, would be welcome. And a break from… It was then I looked at the clock on the car dashboard for the first time. Just gone 1pm. That was consistent with the feelings inside my gut that were telling me, corroborating my sister's generally cheerfully-surprised-if-on-edge state, that we were not late for wherever it was we were headed.

But I knew where we were headed, didn't I?

I caught sight of a petrol station up ahead, coming into view round a bend through the trees that lined this stretch of the dual carriageway.

'I'll stop for some petrol,' I said brightly, lobbing.

'Okay,' in that astonished voice, as if I was asking something of her out of the blue.

'Okay,' I reassured her—everyone—that I wasn't. Point over.

Then we were round the bend and I was indicating and—

'Fucking hell!'

'What?'

'Jesus. The price. How—'

The big digital display read £6.49 for a litre of petrol. There was no display for diesel.

'That's like, bloody hell, more than quadruple what it was on the way here!'

She looked at me then and took a puff of her vape. Some sort of curried cherry?

'What, in the capital?'

The capital? THE CAPITAL? Had I stumbled into an episode of *Last of the Summer Wine*?

'You mean that's normal?'

'Since the government did that thing. I guess. I don't drive now so we don't see it.'

'What thing?'

'Oh I dunno,' she turned to look out the window. 'I don't watch GBNews much.'

She didn't say anything more and I didn't lob. Lobs weren't getting me many returns.

I pulled up at the pump, turned off the engine and got out. It was cold and immediately my hands felt the chill as I opened the petrol cap and took down the pump handle. The pump display sprang to life: modernised, liquid crystal, and a pretty but obviously AI-generated face talking to me.

'Remember to use the gloves provided and sanitise your hands after you've completed the transaction. If you need help, I'm here. My name's Shelly. You're Shelly welcome!'

Christ. £6.49 a litre. Thanks Shelly. I guess that explained the lack of cars.

I was on twenty-five quid before I knew it. Then fifty. For a quarter tank! And it was still going. I stopped around eighty-six. Not even half full. Wow. No wonder she wanted me to pick her up, I thought meanly. The thought cascaded into others, which were memories: that we had, of course, arranged for me to collect her; we had discussed all this in advance; she was expecting me (even if she hadn't been ready). To go to, to go—

I put the petrol cap back on and closed the flap and walked over to the shop to pay. There was no door. I baulked and almost fell over. No door. Okay. At night, maybe, that made sense. In some less salubrious borough of *the capital*. But here, in daylight? I looked again with more attention. Where the shop windows would have been there was a row of touchscreen panels. Above each one a number relating to the pumps. I turned, No.4. And then back, touchscreen 4, and there it was, amber light flashing at me. (4/4, oh yeah! I was right where the universal field wanted me—which suddenly felt ominous). There was Shelly again, full head and torso this time, floating at the side of the touchscreen like a blonde uniformed Casper the Ghost, pointing to various food and drink items on the display.

'Would you like a snack, NY27TYU?' asked Shelly.

Mindreader! I needed something, for sure. I started tapping through to *snacks > healthy snacks > protein bars* and found a range of vegan options, to my enchantment (the marshmallow-cheat-fantasy had subsided). I hadn't asked Kels if she wanted anything. But I knew she'd say no. She wouldn't want to eat in front of me; those waves of bodily shame from our shared childhood still lapped at our feet. I ordered, and my eye caught something move; through dark glass I saw a robotic arm whizz around the shelving and grab my snack bar. Cool, I thought, then winced. Not cool. This was what they'd been warning us about for years: human obsolescence. But why was it taking root out here in yokelland and not in *the capital*? Or maybe it was. The snack bar was vended at the bottom of the screen. I took it and pressed PAY. Shelly was smiling at me with her hands folded over her chest.

'That's £128.65 thank you, first tap your HomeFreedom card, please.'

I didn't know what that was and yet I also did and took my wallet out of my inside suit jacket pocket and found it straight away. It had a picture of my face, serious and round, over a tilted union jack. I tapped it against the card reader. The touchscreen display transformed from product display to graphs of my HomeFreedom data.

I had 764 miles remaining in my annual HomeFreedom travel allowance. Annual!

I had 7 county line passes remaining out of an allocation of 10.

I had 3 passenger vouchers left. (In capitals: *PAPERS REQUIRED*.)

My journeys so far this year had resulted in the planting of 65 trees in Guinea-Bissau.

My HRV was 57, a readiness of six out of ten.

I had not used a MetaSocial product in 13.6 hours (this was flashing yellow).

I had not had a booster jab in 6 weeks (amber, like the siren light above the screen).

I had not informed HomeFreedom I was intending to leave The Capital (flashing red), although this was now updating live, apparently, as a bar of white light ran up and down the sides of the display, scanning my biometrics no doubt and other things, perhaps signs of psychological distress. The flashing red reset to green, although a number in the bottom right-hand corner slowly turned from 1 to 2, which filled me with an unknown source of dread. A tiny version of Shelly appeared floating around it with a disapproving face.

'Thank you for updating your HomeFreedom status. Now please pay £128.65.'

I took out a bank card and paid.

'Thank you.' Face looming out of the screen, growing larger. 'You're Shelly welcome.'

'No, *you're* Shelly welcome,' I said, but she didn't like this. The screen flashed at me.

'You would like to make another purchase? Screen wash? Contraceptives? HomeFreedom bumper sticker? Shelly Welcome fridge magnet?!'

I turned and walked off, with Shelly's appeals following me back to the pump, where Shelly appeared again on the liquid display. I avoided her gaze and got in the car. I put the snack bar into the little drinks and utility space behind the gearstick, feeling not hungry at all (as if that ever stopped me before!). Or perhaps I wasn't comfortable eating in front of my sister, either?

'I didn't ask if you wanted anything, sorry.'

'That's okay.'

Bright, astonished. Interaction without eye contact. The best kind!

*

We got back onto the A14 easily—still no cars—and took off, heading for the A12. We didn't speak for a while. I was, I think, in shock. But was that at the price of petrol, the advancing desuetude of the human workforce, a death trap marquee, or the disappearance of my father? To be fair, I should have gotten used to the latter, him being missing for fifteen years. Was this any different? Well, of course it was. We were there, in the bar. Then we weren't. Then inside the marquee I seemed to have slipped across the universal field as simply as if I'd been out walking and stood on a patch of ice, ending up a few years further along the path. A lost stitch in the weft of instance, a few bumps to show for the ordeal. I believed this could happen. Although I hadn't expected it to happen to me. A related but alternative answer, of course, was that I *hadn't* driven my father out to the coast. Rather, my grief had imagined it for me as distraction on the drive to collect my sister. Perhaps those Ayahuasca ceremonies had altered my brain chemistry so that I experienced my imagined world as real? Was I still doing what my father (had) and sister (still) did, but which (I believed) I'd grown out of? Had I spun myself a story to avoid an intractable unhappiness? But I mean, if I had, *so what*? Wasn't that the *point* of stories? Didn't we lose ourselves through, immerse ourselves in, suspend our disbelief over (*eighty foot over* the English Channel) the stories we told ourselves, exactly so we *could* avoid things like pain, grief, death—reality? The thing I managed to do, I consoled myself, was not to get *stuck* in the narrative. I didn't believe it; I knew it was fiction. This is what it is to be sane: to know the difference. To retain a sense of self, a vantage point of being consciously in touch with reality, to recognise the story as *just* a story. But that's not to say it isn't profoundly shaping. It has its role. And that role, story's role, is psychic preparedness. To learn through story so as to imagine, and imagine a *response*. So that later on, with a resilience built through having repeated it enough times in one's mind, like practice landings in a flight simulator, one can more readily face the true reality of life with a useful response (land the plane). The story as a simulator for truth, but not the truth itself. Isn't that it?

The part about the story not being true, but a psychic preparation for life, a way to develop emotional skills—*that* was the part of it my father and sister had lost touch with. *Shoulda' called you Judas.* No, it wasn't a bloody joke! *Every bone in her body.* Didn't happen! But then...*Wakey, wakey!* Did that happen? Planetary heat death? Was *that* happening? Well, yes it was. But, think then! Had I conjured this story? (You answer that.) Who said it best: Baudrillard? Neo?! Hawking?!! Murdoch?!!! (Iris, not Rupert.) Wasn't 'real life' the illusion? Weren't we all tiny waves acting like particles in the programming of a grand simulator, making the universe up as we went along? Flaps down! Coming in hot!

'Whoa!'

I blinked and pulled the car off the rumble strip. Jesus. The concrete central reservation was not an illusion, not up close.

'Sorry!' I shouted, then calmer, 'sorry.'

With one hand on the steering wheel I used the other to rub my face. My sister was vaping, looking forward through the windscreen. A waft of curried... raspberry masala?

I left the philosophising and concentrated on the road. Ahead of me was the Orwell Bridge (*1984*! Thought crime!) and what looked like a toll booth. I screwed up my brow, another of those unknown knowns slithering its way into my mind.

I slowed as we approached. Two lanes, both unmanned, with large screens the same size as Shelly Welcome's order board, on both driver and passenger sides. Off to the left I noticed an operating room with big windows and real people in grey uniforms.

At the screen I wound down my window. My sister did the same at hers. I was staring into the eyes of another AI-generated face who looked, I felt, a bit like Shelly's gone-off-the-rails banged-up brother. I threw a glance at my sister; her screenface was female.

'Present your HomeFreedom card,' they said in unison. With afterthought, 'please.'

I got the card out of my jacket pocket and looked for where to tap it. Behind me, my sister's border avatar was speaking to her. Where to tap? I noticed Bazza Welcome losing patience, so I wafted it at the screen. 'Thank you.' He didn't smile. My data was on display again, although this time like one of those computer programmes that scrolls past like film credits on speed. Then something flashed and the screen went blank.

Bazza's mug was back. 'Wait here. Do not attempt to drive.'

There was no barrier blocking the way as had my dad's crutch for the Fash. (He had done that, hadn't he?) I suppose some people *did* try to make a scram for it. But dread weighed me down, thinking, knowing, that somehow I'd done something awful in the last few hours and I was about to be confronted with its consequences.

'Oh,' said my sister. Her screen was waving a *Goodbye*. 'Are you not up to date?'

'Have I ever been?' trying to make a joke of it.

Was now the moment to share with her my experiences of the last few hours? Would she understand? Help me make sense of it? I mean, she didn't even really want to be—. I mean, or have him come to her—. I didn't have a clue about any of it; didn't want to, either, this wasn't for me, *it wasn't meant for me!,* I felt very strongly about that, as I had in the terrible marquee; somehow I'd found myself in a temporality that was a simulation, but we still had time to avoid rotten developments, familial and global, it was all a big mistake, I'd left home in 2023 when we still had, what, *two* years left to act, just enough time to drive our decrepit and disappointed but very much alive dad to, well, *her*— not her to *hi*—

'Sir,' said someone. Not Bazza. It startled me.

'What?' I turned. 'Sorry. Officer. Officer?'

This was no angel, *a la* Murvan the Manifest, gun-toting sheriff of the Frederickson and Lane frontier. Bazza in real life. An armed guard was leaning in through the open window.

'Can I see your HomeFreedom card, sir.'

Noted, not a question. I handed it over.

He asked for my name and date of birth and home address, checking it off against the card. He looked at the image and at my face, both serious and both round. He walked to the front of the car and stared at the number plate. He asked me to pop the bonnet, which I did, but only after asking my sister to do so because the handle for it was in her footwell, but she couldn't work it, so I had to awkwardly lean across her lap and get far too close to her knees and calves, close enough to see the veins through the 'savannah caramel' denier of her tights. I popped the bonnet and he opened it and I assumed checked for the chassis number. 'And the boot,' he asked. I popped. He came back to the window.

'What's this?'

I looked at it.

'It's an orange rope.'

He smiled. My, what big teeth you have.

'I know it's a rope. Orange. What's it for?'

What it was *for* was for a friend, who'd scaled the Department for Environment and Rural Affairs building in London as a protest against new coal licenses for the big death pit in Cumbria, when I'd given her a lift to *The Capital*. That particular orange rope had been surplus to requirements. (See, daddio, I told you I knew they'd be on the M25). But I wasn't going to tell him that.

'My boat,' I said. 'The midline. Got it for my boat. A canal boat. To tie up.'

He scrutinized my face. I thought, determinedly, *your data can't see my lie.*

But could it?

He walked away and threw the rope back in the boot and slammed it shut.

'Sir, when did you leave The Capital?'

The Capital! Christ. *Last of the Fascist Summer Wine. 1984! Run for it, Winston!*

'This... this morning...?'

He picked up on my uncertainty. He turned and tapped the screen.

His took his hand off the handle of his gun and whizzed his fingers over the display. What appeared was a slightly fuzzy video of my car passing over the Orwell Bridge in the other direction. I was too far away and his shoulders were too broad to see any detail, such as a time stamp, or *whether I had a passenger*. I watched him rewind and fast forward a few times simply by swiping left and right, pulling the screen apart to zoom in. He double tapped and it went blank. Had I passed the test? Yes! See! We *had* driven over the bridge this morning. Aha! But then—

'Purpose of your journey?'

'Um. To collect my sister.'

I hitched a thumb towards her. Smiled.

'And now?'

Would I say it? Did I know? I did know.

It *was* the universal field. I *had* slipped across years.

But, also, it *was* a diversionary story to avoid the grief. He *had* died.

Did the two have to be mutually exclusive? Wasn't it, at the quantum level, like the alive-and-dead cat of Mr Schrödinger, both *me-slipped* and *me-grieving* at the same time? That's why they christened it the *universal* field! It all existed! It was only now the guard was observing me through the window that one of those universes had come into being, *this* one; or rather, both were now running parallel, but the I in this one was the one who had slipped, and the I in the other was taking his dad to a different funeral. A wave of regret overcame me. So I got *this* universe? After fifteen years of not seeing him, by god, then finding him, him still being so fucking disappointed in everything, in *me*, and drinking, a drunk, but I Capital-A Adulted it, I stiffed it out, I took him for the Guinnesses, I told him things, I asked him things, I found out, I drove him here, all that, all that, but we weren't done, I was *not* done, I still had *so mu*—

'We're off to our dad's funeral,' said my sister, the finality of it floating over my shoulder with that confusing concoction of nicotinic fruit and curry. 'I registered it on my card. See.' She was holding out her HomeFreedom plastic. 'My fault, sir, I forgot to tell my brother he had to as well. He's a bit disorganized.' She vaped, then added, 'he's a writer.'

*

I suppose underneath it all was a buried well of love. But we don't go digging for wells often, when we can turn on a tap of endorphins, or pick up a six-app from—you get the idea. It's a lot of work to dig. But even if you don't, the wells upwell anyway. Like Old Faithful, and you never quite know when it's going to vent a spume and leave you soaked. Strange to think that people plan holidays around such experiences; craving to have anticipation satisfied in unexpected ways (*when will it gush, daddy? I don't know, sonny!*). My well gushed in my dreams. The *two cream doughnuts* premonition I saw not so much as a warning, but as a tapping on my shoulder, the universe giving a knowing nod. It reminded me of the last dream I'd had where my sister appeared; she *did* tap me on the shoulder. I bumped into her (in the dream) after she'd been on an Emerald City Self-Assertiveness Weekend with twenty other women. I bumped into these women crossing a busy street, and she'd tapped me on the shoulder to say hello. One of the other women took a shine to me, and my sister introduced us, saying '*Would you believe he's my little brother?*', a line I overheard her saying to friends at her real (ah, but *was* it *real?*) wedding. Anyhow. The woman (in the dream) who'd taken a shine to me walked off too, but her classmates berated her: hadn't she just taken a class in assertiveness?! Wasn't she now a sparkling facet of The Emerald City?! She returned and jewelly gushed: told me she loved me and we were to have a relationship. I was disconcerted to see she was wearing the same white loose t-shirt my sister had worn in the swimming pool that single time I could recall from our childhood down on the caravan park, to hide her rolls of fat from the other kids. With a half-glance of this woman's breasts inside the dangling wet top, I was, though, won over; and although I didn't find her that attractive at first, slowly we—

Why was I remembering all this?

Well (*well!*) because my sister *was* sitting next to me, and dream-memories were welling up from somewhere, unbid. I'd forgotten the dream up to that point. It was interesting to think I may have had the dream in an entirely different universal field. But it came to me now because, yes, my sister was beside me in the car, but also because I knew that we fool ourselves into thinking the well remains buried. That they won't gush if we don't go digging. Because they do. In dreams, yes. But not only. And dreams are no place to do one's living. Loving is wasted in a night time's fantasy. As incredible as my nightly dreams often were, they were, I understood, no replacement for the messy but lived, the actualised said and done, regardless of whichever of the infinite worlds it was that I happened to be bumbling through at the time. That's perhaps why the dreams gushed: to spume, yes, but to carry us *beyond* the dead and buried. To wake us up on the waterslide of reality. Yes, beyond... that's where the action was.

We were out of Suffolk and into Essex then, passing through the villages I'd noted on the way in: Dedham Vale then Ardleigh, and in quick succession Messing, Feering, and Crix. I *had* been with my dad; I was sure of it. Bazza Welcome and The Armed Guards (Friday's rock and roll band at The Swan, a guest appearance from blonde bombshell Sister Shelly) hadn't commented on passengers in the video he'd checked. But I was certain: we'd been together that morning and years ago. The marquee really had been both an immersive piece of environmental art and slippage into a parallel life. I'd been both soaked by the seawater and gushed upon (metaphorically) by some old geyser. (Dad joke! Who would've guessed?)

I was calmer then, having made sense of the situation. In fact, I was probably too calm. A bit floaty for being in charge of a car and driving at eighty miles per hour. I was, in fact, probably most bothered *not* by having lost my father without saying a proper goodbye; *nor* by somehow losing years of my already too short life; *nor* that I'd quantum leaped past the window that we'd collectively been given to act so as to avoid the very worst of the collapsing climate. No. What I was most bothered by, in my floaty half-dreamt what-the-hell-is-happening humours, was the fact I just could not pin down the aromas of my sister's vapour.

'What flavour *is* that?' I asked next time she took a battery-assisted puff.

'Cardamom and camachile,' she said.

And there was me thinking she and Gavin didn't venture beyond battered cod and mushy peas.

Now that was resolved, other things worrying me were, in no particular order:

Where was I driving to?

What the fuck had happened to Britain?

Had my father *actually* broken every bone in my sister's body in *this* universe?

There was no confusion now, at least, of *where* we were heading. And as my two lives from different fields overlaid each other, I began to recognise memories from this timeline. One of those memories wafted a location at me like a breeze brought in on fanned palm leaves: *Croydon Crematorium, West Chapel.* I only had to play a little game with my sister to confirm it. Although something else was niggling at me then, something that this overlaying of Venn circles had, well, overlooked.

'Thanks for that,' I said, 'covering for me with the guards. Back at the…'

'That's okay,' she vaped.

'Look, I think I know the way there. Croydon Crematorium.'

No shocked response. Okay, good. Keep Calm and Croydon On.

'But I've lost my phone, so… no map. If we need…'

'Sure, we can use mine,' and on cue she took it out of her jacket pocket and stared at the screen for a while, forgetting I was there. I drove on, heading now for the Dartford Crossing, wondering, having seen the price of petrol, how much the Dart Charge was going to be. Fifty-eight quid? A hundred?

My sister's story deserves contextualisation, although I was uncertain that what I knew of her in the other field's history still held true in this one. But what *I* knew was this: she never got on with school much, and as the older sibling, took the brunt of our parents not knowing how to parent. She was older when our father left, five or six, cognisant of the rip; whereas I, a toddler, experienced the tearing without the double-bubble of consciousness to portent. She not only carried the weight of the A.C.E.s but also the heavy-boned genes of our mother's family; and of course, our mother's intergenerational trauma of having given up her first born to adoption. My sister, then, without it ever being said so, had maybe always felt a replacement. Not actually first born. And she was a fat kid. We both were. But as a boy, I got away with it—I didn't have the shame of not adhering to society's sexualised imagery. I grew taller too. There were outlets for me to shift some of that fat, such as sport and lifting weights, which were not, due to that little thing called patriarchy, open to her. Then my sister was bullied at school both by other kids and at least one teacher—male, he mocked her menstruation—and from the age of fourteen she began dressing in the morning in her uniform to leave for school, but in fact spent her days in the park round the corner with other desultory and sad skivers. That's where she began smoking. I guess when she could, she also came home during the day to watch *Judge Judy* and other daytime procrastinations (but not ingressing through the oversized cat flap; she was too old and too big for that). She hid at home, pigged out on Nestlé misshapes and broken biscuits our mother bought on the cheap from the Satanic mill, and then she'd leave again before my mother, stepfather, or I came home. By the time it was exposed, she'd missed too much school, and didn't go back. She left with no qualifications, and drifted through her teens with few friends. She seemed to get mentally stuck at that age, split off into separate parts of herself, as her body matured and became obese, teeth rotted on da Pepsi (the executives of whom should be up there—*strung* up there—with the Big Oil lobby) while her capacity for life levelled out around Madonna and neon pop socks and terrible boyfriends with buttoned-up denim shirts and unskilled jobs in packaging. She wasn't able to think farther than that—too painful. And then, as our mother's own A.C.E.s caught up with her, the two of them drifted placidly into co-dependence, and my sister became our mum's lifelong carer. Kels never left home until aged fifty, and only then because she ran out of parents to feed and wipe. Gavin, her husband with the comics, came along and slipped into the reclining-shaped silhouette that the dead had left. He was at all levels another body and mind in need of repair, but that's another (and not my) story.

Which all made me want to feel bold again, as I had for a moment with our father on the drive out, in those moments of camaraderie after the Battle of the Fash. I wanted to be Capital-A enough to talk with my sister about the things we'd shared, and not do everything I could to avoid them, like make jokes (or use brackets) or stay in my head counting down the minutes until the ordeal would be over. Because what else was it *for*, a car journey on the way to a parent's funeral, if not to confront childhood truths? Surely, I hadn't survived a slip across the universal field to be a coward about these things? Rather, had I not been sent into this future to help bring my sister's Inner Child to integration? Had I not arrived to heal her younger self, the one who'd been split off in that bedroom with the graffitied door that was always locked on the hurtful world, so she could enjoy her Jive Bunny medleys and many other examples of abysmal taste in 1980s music, in peace?

Ah. I'd understood what was niggling me, as the overlaying circles of Venn became one thick-lined sphere. If the 'I' (from the other universal timeline) was now here, in this universal timeline, as 'me', had 'I' just landed on and splatted the 'me' who was already here? I suppose that counted as more than a niggle: was it some sort of flattening manslaughter, a timeline auto-cide? Or did it count, and I supposed this might be just as reasonable a conjecture, as further psychotic distraction from the grief of losing a last living parent. Hey? The question was, how did one tell such hypotheses apart? Which *was* the most likely answer?

*

Eighty-seven quid. (The Dartford Crossing.) But there was no traffic and we were making good time. The counties of Essex and Kent clearly had some sort of Schengen arrangement as we didn't have to tap in our HomeFreedom cards, nor have Bazza Welcome frown forebodingly at my dumbstruck non-sequiturs. Was I getting used to this future already? My sister explained as we cranked up the lobbing once more that the Dartford Crossing was so well monitored that they didn't need the *extra* security, and that borders had only been drawn between those areas with a coastline and the next inland county. Since the 'flood' (she did indeed use the word 'flood' and for a moment I thought she was referring to sea level rise, but alas, no), since the 'flood' had found ingenious ways to overwhelm the coastal borders, the Home Office Minister (who sounded like a Tory, although apparently the 'reds' won the last 'official' election) had announced this next line of defence. I nodded along.

'Don't you know all this?' she said.

'I thought you didn't watch the news?' I deflected.

Vape. 'The girls in the post office like a chat. And you can't help see the front pages of the newspapers when you have to do the wrap and return.'

They still had news*papers*. Fair enough.

'Fair enough,' I repeated, for her benefit.

We were past Sutton at Hone now, and coming up on Lullingstone. I couldn't help noticing how much softer the place names in Kent were, how much more Edenic than Essex.

'What did you mean by *official*, by the way,' I asked. 'About the election.'

She looked sideways at me.

'Pretend I don't know.'

She shook her head.

'No, no, no. You're trying to trick me into saying something. You're much cleverer than I am, you watch the news.'

Her fear was real. I shook my head too. Not at her claims of educational inferiority—which were mostly true; what was the point of denying it, as much of a wanker as that made me sound—but more by the fact I'd become derailed from the task of digging for wells by the politics of the day (whichever day it was). Easily done when you've missed an electoral cycle.

'I'm not, I promise. I'm,' oh, that little dig from earlier. I smiled, 'I'm a writer, after all!'

Vape. Vape.

I wasn't convincing her.

'It's good to hear,' I began on another tack. 'I don't get to hear what the ladies at the post office think, and that's not good. Not good to be in your little bubble, is it? Silo.'

'Who's Si Low?'

'I mean, you know, algorithms, Facebook. When we only hear from people who always read the same papers. If we all think the same way. What was not *official* about it?'

She shrugged. She'd never really used Facebook. A faint hope wafted by: that in this timeline Zuckerberg had been successfully sued for his intellectual property theft and the algorithm's disregard for teenage life. To within an inch of his barricaded Hawaiian mansion. One can hope; but one expects that most possible outcomes are a sad version of the same. Anyway, what was my sister saying?

'Say that again?'

'Well, Nigel didn't accept... You know, the bad counting. All that ID fraud. It was stolen, wasn't it? That's what a lot of the girls...'

Fucking hell, I thought. So *that's* what happened to Britain. Trumplandia-on-Sea.

Which made me admire The Badger Liberation Army even more.

Oh, but. Different timeline. So,

'Do you—'

But anything I was going throw at her that I knew to be true back in my universal field, such as, and I quote, *the net positive contribution made to the economy* by that 'flood', might *not* be here. Or if it had been, was it now, in this future I'd skiddingly and without much

grace slippaged into? Had things deteriorated so much, so quickly?
 Well, possibly, yes. It looked like they had.
 But I wouldn't let it go, would I?
 'Your work colleagues believe that, do they?' I asked, an aside at the wonder of how the post office was still operating. I guessed people did even more of their shopping online and the parcel service had survived.
 'Well no-one's proved it wasn't stolen.'
 Hmm. I rubbed my brow, and it felt hot. I carried on around the M25, this particular articulated future free from those pesky Just Stop Oil protesters, who had either all *given* up or been *banged* up (I knew which my money was on). We drove on past Well Hill (*!*) and Badgers Mount (*!!*) keeping an eye out for the signs to Croydon. All the while, I was trying to strategize how I could first of all confront these reactionary ideas that scared the people in seafront towns, counting among their number my living sister, ideas which they cultivated amongst themselves (the girls at the post office like to— the boys in the yacht club, too), although eased along of course by the right-wing media, who painted their coastal homes as the frontline—the *flood*line—of the battle to Make Britain Great. Could I persuade my sister that *stopping the boats* full of brown people was not in fact the way to fix an overwhelmed NHS, nor were the brown people stealing their post office jobs; and *then,* if I could do that, could I also perform a successful segue into a gentle but necessary exposing of my sister's *real* wounds? Could I reveal to her the *real* things that scared her: not brown people, not iffy untruths about stolen elections, but the older, more banal and universal harms buried deep down, of a frightened Inner Child who was, in her fifties now, treading water, those waters being where the *real* (psychological) flood had taken place. The well had upwelled and drowned her from the inside. It was these *real* unhealed traumas that kept her grasping for a float in the shape of a TV remote, anything to keep her above the waterline, a fastened thing to grab to; but in doing so, she was having her blowholes of anxiety exploited and redirected by the Alt-Govt and MediaFash towards more fruitful

(for them) targets (and didn't they know it.)

'Have you ever felt safe?' I asked. Not sure where that came from, but it was a start.

And I suddenly thought: *that's projection.* Have *I* ever felt safe?

She shook her head.

'Oh no. When you see the boats...' and she carried on, like a propaganda tickertape with a life of its own. Yet that was the MediaFash's greatest success, wasn't it, at the behest of Corruption Capitalism, to coerce people into thinking that their traumas came from the Unknown Other out there, and *not* from fears much, much closer to home. How was I going to counter that Great Ingrained, in one car ride? Even with the heightened emotional proclivities of being on the way to our father's funeral.

Silence. I wondered what she'd said. If I'd been less of a Si Low myself, I supposed, if I'd been listening, I would have learnt something about her, and been able to respond.

'Why did you decide to come, in the end?' I asked her. 'To his...'

Back in the other timeline, when I'd attended her wedding, she was absolutely positive she *wouldn't want him here* hadn't wanted him there. To recap: she'd called our mum's third husband *dad*. (And buried him no problem.) When I'd hired the PI to find our father after his fifteen-year disappearing act, she didn't want to know *couldn't face it* my aunt relayed the message to me (oh god. Was Auntie still alive *here*?). My sister's A.C.E.s had not been processed, the past *inner work capable of facing him* unworked, the well, *well*, well and truly, blown. Bodies under the rubble! *When will it gush, daddy?* Ah, fuck the old geyser!

'I know,' she replied, 'but,' *vapépeuse,* 'but he's still dad—'

She welled up, but stoppered it there.

Water flooded the corners of my eyes too.

It was simple, after all, wasn't it, this thing. Love.

But could I leave it? Cease and desist in peace? R.I.P.? Of course not! R.I.P. it up!

Because, what about the lies? What about the *every bone in her body*? Or *your mother tried to smother you with a pillow*? Maybe my sister, who had been older, knew the veracity of these things. Maybe she'd been there for the family wrap and return and hadn't been able to help herself from reading the parental headlines? Perhaps this was the only chance I'd have to discover if they were true or not. Had our father really been that much of a bastard? Or, had he told his story the way the MediaFash did, the way most of us knew how to, which was to create a line that reinforced what he needed to hear: in his case, a shaky sense of self. These stories they made up, my sister and my dad, were attempts to make sense of an unsafe world. Something certain they could go by, even if it not true. But at least the story was *theirs*. It couldn't be challenged, not really (another Trumplandism, I noted). It was, for all intents and purpose, a reliable history. A story that they could depend on when all other stories fell away. And once they'd repeated it enough times, it became theirs, became *them*. It didn't matter if it was based on a lie. A lie will do, *as long as it tells us who we are*. Which is, in the end, perhaps all they ever wanted. To know who they were.

I say *they*. I mean *us*. *All* of us.

And you. And both me-s. All the me-s in the universal field!

Yet: could we unravel this mess of truth and lies together, my sister and me? Reach a new peak of understanding? What an achievement that would be! Practically, virtually, in every universe *except this one* an impossible feat; and yet, wasn't this collective healing what we needed? I smugly, most likely smugly, congratulated myself for reaching this conclusion, prior to testing even a word of the theory; not saying it, but formulating what I would say, holding back with exquisite painful glee, words best kept under wraps to maintain their perfection. But no, the speech was on its way! I must gush! Effervescing in my mind, fizzing on my tongue, spurting across the airwaves.

If I had had more empathy in me at that moment and less surety (and less simile), if I hadn't been thinking of my own healing and the need to show it off, if I hadn't been blindsided by the sharp exit from the M25 onto the B269 at Titsey (god's honest!) and careered out of control and through a gap between two old elm trees and into a shallow ditch that saved us from crashing into a fence, I might even have thought to ask my presumed wounded sister a genuine question, rather than postulate my self-aggrandizing conclusion in throbbing car-crash philosophy.

Not, *What I think is this:*
But, *What happened to you?*

*

We came to a bumpy stop. The car lay flopped but not overturned in the ditch, and we lay both slumped and not overturned in the car. There had been oohing, shouting, and other strange sounds, sounds you wouldn't expect to hear unless you had put a car into a trench at sixty miles an hour. Only then do you discover what is emitted in such a scenario.

My head was hurting. I put a hand to my forehead and looked at the hand. No blood, but there had been pain. I grabbed the mirror and adjusted it for a better look and saw a large lump forming in real time. Another strange noise; my sister. Her body had not been in my peripheral vision. Which I thought was interesting. The majority of perceptual signals travel *not* from the eye to the brain, but *from the brain to the eye*, creating in advance an expectation of what we see out there, and only registering difference between the prediction and the actual. Which meant that my brain—but *which* brain? *which* timeline?—had not expected my sister to be in the car. Anyway, probably what was needed was not *more* philosophising about brain mechanics in temporal dimensions, but a focus on a real live sister.

'Shit. Are you—?'

She was.

'I'm okay.' She was hugging herself. 'What happened?'

'I just took the exit too fast. Sorry. I wasn't expecting it.'

Titsey, for god's sake.

'Are you okay? That's a big lump.'

My god, my heart, she can see my heart. But ah. Just my head.

'It does hurt. I guess I smacked it?'

'Is the car alright?'

'I dunno.'

The engine had stalled. I thought about getting out and checking the car, but actualising the thought was beyond me. The steps overwhelming. Seat belt, door, no chance. I sat listening to things settle, the creak of a bit of metal, the sinking of a tyre.

'I'll look,' she said, managing more than me, taking the steps to unbuckle, open, get out. Unhurt, thank god. Imagine having set out that morning in another timeline to transport my dad to my sister's funeral, only to slip across the universal field into a new future to find her still alive, but then kill her in a car crash. Ironic!

The car tilted a little, but we seemed stable enough. She walked around the car's edges, hugging her black jacket to her, vaping away as she inspected the scene. She was being more competent than I, more competent than I had assumed her to be, which was the story of her life of course. I understood, then, that it was not my job to go digging for wells or worms; if she wanted to do her own digging, then that was down to her, as mine had been down to me; rather, I was to play my part in building whatever relationship we could in the present (whatever present we were given) on whatever ground was under us. If it was shaky, fine! A little ditchy in Titsey? No problem! The more realistic the better, I guessed, under these particular circumstances. (Were there ever circumstances that *weren't particular*? Don't ask me. I had a bump to the head caused, quite directly, by *too much philosophy*.)

Another car came towards us, a Mercedes, one of those rakish two seaters you see a lot in these parts of the country, those with an overabundance of detached houses, boundary fences, and whinnying horses. The driver pulled up fifty yards further along the road in the gravel bend of a driveway. He got out and walked towards us. He was wearing a wide brimmed hat and a lumbering Barbour jacket. Right then I would have given anything in the world to be able to scream, Look at his fucking red trousers!, but alas, they were brown or black (but corduroy? still at least corduroy?!). My sister had spotted him and now they were talking, arms waving, although my sister continued to pin her jacket to her chest. She turned and pointed her vape at me. The gentleman took his hat off to reveal thick locks of blond-grey hair. He must have been sixty, I thought, well-lived, blood type CEO, most likely well-loved by mama and papa, who were both still alive and squishing grapes with their feet on the *gîte* in Bordeaux.

I squinted. Yes, a Mercedes. Corduroys. I was a fucking judgemental one, wasn't I? Even in distress. Even with the evolving lump. Not my fault though, right? It was my upbringing! Trained to be hyper-vigilant! What was it Doris Lessing said about stressed childhoods making writers of observant children? I box breathed in, *appreciation*, out, *love*, in, *appreciation*, out, *surrender*. I hoped once round the meditative square might mellow me.

Mr Mercedes knocked on my driver's door window and smiled.

'Hellooo,' he shouted through the glass, bending down with hands splayed on his *brown* corduroys covering his masterly thighs. 'That's a bastard junction, as you've just discovered.'

I nodded. Judgements aside, I was mightily relieved to be in his purview.

'You in one piece, chap?'

I wound down the window. *Eau de Boss* wafted in.

'I think so. Bang on the head.'

He inspected the bump, looking down his nose from a number of angles.

'Quite a thud. You'll probably be concussed. Can't drive.'

'No,' I agreed, shaking my head. My first competent thought (all day? ever?!) was *I've failed again, thank god, failed again to get to anyone's funeral*. If the tree falls in the forest but there's no one there to hear it, does it make a sound? If we never make it to the funeral to see off the dead, does anyone really die?

I asked Mr Mercedes, our cheerful Good Samaritan, what he made of that. He frowned, tilted his head to scrutinize my face, then stood up, wiping his hands on his jacket pockets as if the interaction had been a bit greasy.

'Can't drive,' he shouted to my sister, who was, scrutably, standing some way off.

'No!' my sister shouted back, shaking her head. 'He can't!'

They smiled at their common understanding.

'Well, can you?' he shouted.

She nodded and grunted. Tonal. So tonal! Proof we were related! He understood.

'Well, the car's not damaged by the looks. Seems you'll be okay.'

'I'll get him to the funeral, don't you worry,' she shouted back.

Our Good Samaritan's face! I'll never forget that look: a lifetime of taking charge slipped into shocked alarm at this announcement, his eyes as wide as the Grand Canyon. (Which is, out of interest, exactly 867 miles from that spurting geyser Old Faithful on the I-15, passing many wonderfully named places, my favourite being Duck on a Rock; now there's a lookout point to reference in parenthesis if you, too, have to distract yourself from getting to a funeral.) I tried to laugh at my bracketed narrative—one more of my many attempts at diversion from the purpose at hand!—but it hurt my ribs. My eyes went wobbly.

'That's where we were heading,' I said, hoarsely out the window. 'To a funeral.'

'Our dad's,' added my sister, now surprisingly close.

'Oh,' said our Good Samaritan. 'Oh!' And laughed, then realised what he was laughing at. He forced a frown but it didn't last long, and we all chuckled along. 'Well...'

Well, well, indeed! Well up! Well done! Well played! Well gushed!

'Get him to the funeral!' I muttered, no doubt sounding hysterical. Mr Mercedes and my sister looked at each other in a knowing fashion; the bump had, to them, made me talk about myself in the third person. Together they opened my door, unbuckled my belt, lifted me out. They hobbled me around to the passenger's side as if they were my crutches, one under each armpit. The Good Samaritan smelled of peaches and custard, but I wouldn't tell you the story of what childhood trauma flashed through my memory right then, even if you paid me. The Good Samaritan swung open the car door and they heaved me down and I rested my head and breathed very slowly.

For a moment, in the peace, I was sure I heard the echo of a rattling pair of lungs.

But nah, nahimbaemae, it wasn't. It couldn't be.

/ Bye, dad.   Bye. \

'Nearly COP'D it,' I said, and giggled. The pair of them outside laughed too, although at a different joke.

'Nearly copped it indeed,' said the GS. 'But you're alright. What time's your funeral?'

The question set me off laughing. Jesus, my ribs!

'In which universe? They're scheduled at different times.'

Our rescuer was confused, and, rather impertinently, shut the door on me. Probably for the best. I heard my sister thank him again, then they shook hands, and he walked back to his car parked fifty yards up the road. My sister took her time to get around to the driver's side and stood on the road for a moment taking three, four, five calming lungfuls of cardamom and camachile. It was then that I noticed the number plate on our Good Samaritan's Mercedes. And I joke you, kid you, mock you not, it was 44 ANG.

Hark!

*

We shunted the car out of the ditch and were on our way. Having my sister drive was almost as frightening as being trapped in that ever-shrinking tunnel of the black marquee. I see now why she and Gavin had sold their car: not to save on petrol, but as a public service. *Tear along the dotted line* took on a whole new meaning.

But then *I'd* been the person who crashed us off the M25, hadn't I?

We were close now. We passed through places I remembered as a child. Coulsdon, Farthing Downs, Waddon. A place off Coulsdon High Street, venue to the Kids' Christmas Club, an afternoon of awkwardness in what felt like both a completely empty and at the same time overwhelmingly packed crowd of bigger kids. Next, the fake-Tudor-beamed public house where we would arrange to meet with my stepmother's sons and their mates (they who teased me as The Icebox) as we formed a convoy of cars (caval-*what*?) heading to Selsey Bill's caravan park. They were exciting days, regardless of the general state of fear we lived in at our father's inconsistent love and rage. I looked across to see if these places registered with my sister. I wanted to say something, share something, but the shock of ending up in a ditch, while wearing off, kept me pinioned to the seat. I did note, though, she was driving without her phone. Following her internal map of past years or road signs. Either way: competent.

My head was pounding, and in a particularly exquisite throb another memory came back to me: of hitchhiking in Australia after college and answering an ad on a hostel noticeboard. Someone needed a driver going south. I answered. He sold himself as a bona fide Hells Angel (angel!), Queensland Chapter. He sort-of looked the part. About 5'7" with straggly, greasy greying hair, and a black Megadeth t-shirt cut off at the shoulders under a bebadged and torn denim jacket, also sleeveless. Skinny, melanomaed forearms with random, fading, purplish tattoos. A cigarette permanently dangling from a chapped lower lip, pierced eyebrow (and nipples, it turned out. Wince). Truly, a fallen angel had come to rescue me from the dire financial straits I'd found myself in. The Subaru estate that my gap year buddy and I had bought in an underground car park from a group of Swiss travellers (the Swiss! Neutral! Who knew they could be so devious?) had blown up not once, but twice. We whooshed away our entire gap year's money in six weeks. My buddy went home to England, his dream of surfing Oz in pieces. I, who'd joined the trip without much of a plan, decided, well, I was here now, so what's the worst that could happen? With my belief in the superposition of the natural order emboldened by a set of mystical beads bought from a cute blonde in hippie mecca Byron Bay, how could I refuse the offer to journey south from one of hell's angels?

So we were off. I was expecting to be cruising on a Harley (not that I could ride a bike) or at the very least some sort of hot rod, a souped-up Camaro or Dodge Charger. I was underwhelmed by the Datsun Cherry, but hid my surprise from Mr HA, who turned out to be a touchy fella. He'd had his licence taken off him for drunk driving and assaulting a police officer, had the black eye to show for it. He needed a chauffeur to get him and his hot cherry back to Sunshine Coast. He didn't want to risk driving himself. And yet when we were underway, he turned paranoid, berating me for driving at 109kph one kilometre per hour under the speed limit, and then also for 111kph, one over. I sat there stiffly holding the wheel, maintaining pace, driving this gobby Aussie imbecile a thousand miles down the east coast, listening to his stories of sexual or barroom triumph or Sticking It To The Man, stories which in themselves were an education in how not to make a life. The lesson was not quite worth every penny of the blown Subaru engine. And then, as we were driving past a patch of strawberry fields, the M1 motorway fading, as it does in parts of the Australian scrubland, into little more than a wide dirt road, my ride panicked when he saw a car coming the other way carrying two well-dressed men.

'It's the fuzz!' he shouted, 'and you're fucking driving one-one-five!' at which he grabbed the steering wheel, took us off the road and bouncing into the strawberries.

To be honest, if we'd wanted to attract the attention of an undercover police vehicle, careering off the road was probably the way to do it. But my hellish Seraph knew differently. We sat among the strawberries listening to the sounds of a car coming to rest, the fruit not ripe enough to wind down my window and reach out and taste. We stayed for long enough to stop fearing if the fuzz (!) had seen us. Other than the gash a Datsun makes when ploughing through strawberry plants, there was little discernible clue we were there. This stretch of motorway was deserted with 'Warning: Next Gas 200 kilometres' signs every hundred miles.

The fella had a smoke. I sat there, bumped around and a little in shock, but not injured. Knowing, even then, that at some point later in life it would make a good story. (Not knowing, of course, that the time to tell it would be after a similar bump off the road on the way to my father's funeral.) Halfway through his joint, Kid Gabriel began talking, taking mellow swipes at my poor driving.

(Did he offer me any of the joint? Did he f—.) Of course it had been *my* fault for the overzealous speeds I'd been reaching (where had I heard *that* before, hey daddio?). He'd had to act. And if his car was damaged, well, there'd be hell to pay, but he supposed I was a piss poor traveller from England, otherwise why would I be travelling with him, and so, such payment to hell would not be forthcoming. Right? I corroborated this presumption. I had fifty Aussie bucks to see me through a thousand miles. Joint still lit, Hells got out and popped the bonnet and checked over the engine. And I thought, if your spliff's cherry drops and blows the big Cherry, who'll be responsible for this fried patch of strawberry? Me? The undercover fuzz? The fruit farmer? Anyone butt, right?

But we survived, and got the car back on the road without interference. Heading south again with some strange abandon, the Hangel decided he'd drive for a stretch. Fine, I thought, tired of being griped every time I went a kilometre above or below his limit. So I relaxed in the passenger seat after our bump off the highway. And *that's* why I was remembering it now; sister driving, Vape vaping, head resting and eyes staring out of the window at the passing of Purley Oaks and the Way—I was experiencing a buried muscle memory from that earlier off-roading. Then as now, I watched country sail by, the only difference being this present country south of London was not open desert and sky, but made up of rows of fast-food franchises, pawn shops, and ghosts of previous me-s.

Back in Oz: another niggle to the nirvana of our trip together was Hells' music. Bad hillbilly rockaboo, somewhere between Guns N' Roses and Woody Guthrie but with none of the pizazz. INXS without the XS.

The cassette tape came to the end of its side in the stereo.

'Dig another one out, mate,' he said, waggling a finger at the glove box.

Stuffed in there like fading envelopes in the mailbox of the dead were more than two dozen cassettes, mostly loose, a few in their cracked boxes, some shop-bought and some homemade. I waded through. A bunch I'd never heard of (then or again): Australian

Crawl. Boom Crash Opera. Cold Chisel. The Angels! I kept rummaging and pulled out a cassette with stuck on pink glittery stickers and the handwritten legend Salt-N-Pepa.

'Salt-N-Pepa,' I laughed, holding it up mockingly. 'Yours? Not heavy metal is it!'

He looked across at me with venom in his eyes, and a strange panic.

'What the—' he lunged for the cassette but I pulled back out of his reach. He lunged again, and the venom made him aggressive and unavoidable. 'Not fucking mine, that shit. You taking the piss outta me?' A stare, the Cherry wobbled on the road. 'Fucking black girls.'

He grabbed the tape, let go of the steering wheel with his other hand and wound down his window (proper winder, no electrics) and threw the tape onto the highway. I was stunned by the racism, shocked by the aggro, incredulous at the tossing of a tape over, what, a little bit of ribbing? I wasn't sure what had just happened, or why. After he'd wound the window up, he leant across my legs and grabbed a cassette from the still open glove box and slammed it into the tape player and pressed play. And we drove on like that for another hour or so, listening to the synth-rock of Icehouse, who weren't too bad, until my Angry Angel got tired of driving and his fury subsided and he wanted another spliff, so we swapped seats, and he smoked and carried on his mellow sniping at me. I drove us the rest of the way that night, and the next day, down to Sunshine Coast, where we parted ways.

Although before we did, we stayed that night in a weed den, the house of one of his mates. The weed dealer was busy all night selling his crop of bud as his mother-in-law was coming the next day for the weekend, and he'd been ordered by the wife to get all the gear out of the house. In between front-door sales, as I tried and failed to sleep on the sofa, I learnt from his old buddy that Mr Hells Angel was an estranged father. That he had an eleven-year-old daughter whom he saw about twice a year, and would take on road trips. That he'd not seen her for a year or so. The daughter's mother didn't want my ride to have much to do with their child. Fair enough, with his lifestyle, attitude, and misericiousness.

See? That tape. Why I was indulging the long and old memory. Little since had made me as sad as that angry, prideful, beat-up fella throwing his daughter's handwritten cassette tape out of the window. For what? To save face with some teenage Brit who he'd never see again? What a fucking tragedy. It was more important for him to hold a weak grip on this hard-ass Hells Angel pretence than hold onto a gift from his child. What a waste. What sadness. *His* daughter, if she ever got in the car again, would be lied to about her Salt-N-Pepa. The cassette she'd recorded for road trips together. *Some English bugger nicked it,* he might say, not looking at her crestfallen face.

I wished I had. Nicked it. Better than reality.

Better than what this father had done to his daughter.

I was heaved back into the present by a loud car horn and a lurch to the left.

'Sorry,' said my sister.

I looked around. We were on the Croydon Flyover.

Not far now. I supposed it was now or never. For that daughter, for this one. For me.

'Before we get there...'

I wondered if never would be better.

'What is it?'

I rubbed my face, covered my mouth.

Rub the chin, hold the tongue. The old mantra!

But! Surely whatever stories *she'd* stored in *her* hippocampus from our early years would be worse (internalised as they had been by *her* Inner Child) than anything *I* could ask her as an adult? I just needed to wheel out o'l Capital-A, didn't I, and handle it well. (*Well, well!*) I sat up straight in the passenger seat, rearranged my bum, set myself to speak. Wasn't my sister now taking control of the situation, Capital-C Competent, driving us both to a funeral she never wanted to go to anyway but found the decency to do so. If there was ever a moment to reveal the harms and expose the wounds to fresh air, wasn't it while we had *this time now*, in *this* universe? How many of us ever get *another* universe for a shot at it? We were crawling along past the Factory Lane Recycling Centre, not far, within bawling distance, of where we'd both been born, Mayday Hospital. Mayday! Mayday! A call from angels! That was it, the final sign. Wasn't I being silly trying to plug the well? Weren't we soaked already? Wasn't there hope to gush it all once and for ever?

'Did he really break every bone in your body?'

Shit. I said it.

She drove on through traffic lights and round to the left at Thornton Heath pond.

'Who?'

Who? WHO? Amazing. Utterly amazing. Who do you think, sister-o, Murvan the fucking Manifest? Salt-N-Pepa? The Datsun Cherry Mercedes Hells Angels?! *Who*, for fu—

'I'm confused.' Bright, astonished. Vaped.

Capital C-Confused. Was Capital-A Adult in the car, I wondered? I puffed my cheeks.

'Dad.' I paused. 'Your pal Tracy, she told me at the wedding—'

'Who's Tracy?'

'Hey, what?' I tried to frown but the throbbing was too sore for that. 'Your pal, from Iceland. Works with Gavin in the stockroom. She tried to—'

'I don't know any Tracy.'

'Tracy told me that's what you told her. She told me at the wedding.'

'Who's wedding?' she asked.

Oh dear.

Was there Tracy in *this* universal field? In this timeline? (No, I'm not gonna... Okay, I will:) No *trace* of her? (Argh! Too far. Too far with the fucking jokes...)

'I don't know what you're talking about,' said my sister.

And truthfully, I had no idea either. It had shaken her, but then wouldn't it, being asked if your father had done *that*? Whether it was true or not. I breathed deeply, trying to suck up some of her capers and chimichanga, to suck in some of that history from my old mate's flaming cherry. Was my sister lying? Did it matter? Was it any of my business? Hadn't I resolved earlier, immediately after taking the car off at Titsey, with *Look at my fucking brown corduroys 44 ANG* come to show me that *I didn't need to go digging* or *opening* or *diving* or *nothing*. Cans, wells, burials. Had I forgotten the lesson already?

Oh indeed. Not one to learn quickly, me. Not where digging up the truth is concerned.

I needed to know. Was that so wrong? I needed to understand.

'So he never broke every bone in your body?'

She vaped. She vaped again. She wasn't going to answer.

Wiser than me, I thought. And I understood. She *was* telling the truth, for what it was worth, the truth being whatever story she had come to live by, in whichever timeline that made most sense to her. Life made liveable by a storyline of your choice. For instance, this one, for me, in which my dad—older, sick—*had* died, and my sister—younger, with years left to live—was still alive. So, in *this* timeline, *that* thing I'd asked her had never happened.

I felt relief. Something like relief. Maybe happiness, that it had not happened to her.

Oh. But. It hadn't happened to *this* sister.

Grief took me by the gullet, constricted my throat. It was difficult to breathe—for a moment. Because *somewhere*, to some sister of mine, perhaps in that other timeline, it had. To that one. Oh, daddio.

*

'Will you put on the radio?' I asked her once my throat deconstricted.

She looked angry, I thought, or distressed by my condition. Obviously, for her, the bump on my head had led to strange thoughts, the imagining of evil stories and an Iceland stockroom manager of whom there was no— (no, not twice). That's what she was telling herself, and it was a kindness, so I thanked her for it.

'Thank you,' I said.

'I've not done it yet,' she replied. 'We're there now. Why'd you want the radio?'

We were in the middle of the road indicating to turn right into the cemetery.

'I don't know, I just want to listen... please?'

She looked down at the buttons.

'It's your car. Which one?'

I looked down. Blurred, the buttons came into focus. I hit *On* and it burst into life. It took a few bars, but I recognised the song. *Mr Blue Sky*, by ELO. So, in this timeline, this universal field, the ethereal rock of the seventies had happened. I sat and listened. And then,

'*Hey there, Mister Blue, we're so pleased to be with you, look around see what you do, everybody smiles at you,*' I sang along, and my sister, pleased that my brain was working as normally as ever (read into that what you will) suctioned up a valedictory vape.

'Our dad's favourite,' she said.

Oh god. Now *she* wanted to open the can? Was I his fav— Oh, no, she meant—

'Oh, the song.'

Yes, the song. Idiot. So it was.

'*—but sooooon comes Mr Night, creeping over, now his hand on your shoulder, never mind, I'll remem—*'

My sister turned into the driveway and pootled along at not a mile per hour under nor a mile per hour over the ten miles per hour speed limit. Someone was learning! And so she drove us steadily and competently through the graves and into the car park of Croydon Crematorium, West Chapel, where the funeral directors and celebrant were ready and waiting to, well—

The End.

A novel as an alarm clock

(harvesting the collaborative 'scenius' of HardArt)

What is the point of a novel? Of any book, to hold back the collapsing climate? Of a work of art to 'inspire' or at least 'entertain'? What is the point of acquiescing to a publishing industry unwilling to face collapse? Of relying on the whims of commissioners and agents on the hustle to make deals that feed egos, in the hope that we can business-as-usual, hope the huge thing over there *la la la* isn't happening and that there will still be bookshops and pension schemes and copyright acts fifteen years from now? Of ignoring all the stories (*A State of Denmark, Parable of the Sower, The Man in the High Castle*) as 'only stories!' rather than seeing them as oracles of the coming (at best) single-party authoritarian government or (at worst) a world fractured into barbarous tribal factions where your kids will be fighting (literally) for food?

I've wrestled with this. I've bounced around a triangle for what feels all my life (perhaps lives!): I write, but worry I feel self-indulgent; so I push myself into activism on the ground; yet the activism does not change enough, so I turn to theory for answers; but those practices are dusty and they're dull and my soul craves making, so I turn back to imaginative writing that feels, for a while at least, as if it is a truth that comes from where a soul might live. This triangulation continues, although I work to integrate, to find a way to bring them together. It's time consuming. And how do I (do you) know what's even the right thing to do?

I once chaired a panel at the Manchester International Festival where I met the artist Julian Oliver. He combined his knowledge of technology and will to create with a sense of what is being lost. One of his works (collaboratively made with Crystelle Vu) is the *Extinction Gong*, which gongs every nineteen minutes as another species is lost to human extractivism, greed and rapaciousness. In the conversations over those few days and afterwards, I remember Julian's words clearly, indeed gongingly, that all of us, especially artists, need to "live in the time we're in" rather than continue to make art or write books that don't try, at least, to come to terms with the times.

That is one of the questions that drives **HardArt** and some of the people who attend—if you've not read HardArtist Jay Griffiths' explanation of **HardArt** in her beautiful Foreword, please do so. Another Hardist, Gavin Turk, speaks often during the sessions of needing to find out what is the art worth making amidst the crises, the times. It isn't simply a matter of writing or making art 'about' the intersecting shitshow we're living in—although that is part of it. As my old mucker, author, tutor and now friend Nick Royle once said, if we only thought that art was 'about' something we'd all make nothing.

So, what is the point of a novel then? What is the point of this novel? What is the point of imaginative making? Of creating art?

One argument: if we can imagine a different world, maybe we can make it. And if we can't imagine it, we have no chance of making it.

Another argument: people want to create. And what are we trying to save humanity *for* if not to live in creative, peaceful, fulfilling becoming with one another? Is art not a playful, joyful way of being, not through extraction but by honouring the world and its beauty?

Yeah, yeah, all that. But do *I* get to do that, when there's so much urgent work to do?

If I tell some of the story of why I wrote this, it could provide a partial answer.

I've always stood by the necessary creative ethos that together:

form + content = the work. The content of this novel is 'about' aspects of the crises we are facing together. Climate collapse, social collapse, authoritarianism, how to retain the capacity to love and to face the obstacles that stop us from loving. I had to write it for a few reasons:

1. I'd been writing about my father for a long time—when he was missing, and then after he was found (the novel is semi-autobiographical, but remains a work of fiction). Finding him felt like the end of a story which people encouraged me to document. I was writing, but without a form, and without an audience. It felt like a waste.
2. It was at a time when I'd spent too long working on an academic report that was derailed by Covid. I felt stagnant and bored, wanting instead to draw from my well of truth in imaginative ways. I needed to write creatively—I needed to *make*—but I didn't have the time (teaching!) or energy (Long Covid) to do lots of research. In case of creative emergency, make or break out of what is in front of you. I'd just found my dad. So that is what I did.
3. I didn't want to write anything serious. After animal suffering (my *Pig* book) and environmental disaster (*Chernobyl*) and efforts of serious nonfiction (such as a report on plant-based food systems), I wanted to have fun while writing.

And then of course a third of the way into writing, my father died (for real). I didn't really know what to do. A conversation with the writer Liz Jensen, who lost her son Raphaël when he was just 25 which she documents in her incredible memoir *Your Wild and Precious Life*, gave me permission to keep the conversation going with my father. Even if the novel was not 'worth it' in terms of a response (adequate? proportional?) to the intersecting shitshow of climate collapse and the risk of a slide into authoritarian chaos, I finished *Daddio!* as a draft.

Yet, what can a novel do? What was the point of writing when there was so much work to be done—organising, building a movement, mobilising the public to change failing political cultures and to build alternatives that can sustain us through the collapse; indeed, in helping people understand that our systems are already in a state of collapse.

I was bouncing around the triangle.

Yes, but could a *novel* do this work?

Perhaps. I knew books in the past (such as *Black Beauty* or *Silent Spring*) had led to political change. But we live in a different time. Was to "live in the time you're in" a message to abandon creative work and throw myself fully into activism and organising?

I reconsidered: **form + content = the work**.

The first rule of **HardArt** is that it is collaborative. It is through the act of coming together that we can make work that, perhaps, responds to the times we're in, if not adequately or proportionately, at least appropriately. Books, and especially novels, are the site of 'genius' *par excellence* and feed the myth of individual excellence, the image of the sole creator working alone. There *is* a lot of time spent alone; time sought alone, too, for the maker who wants control, who wants to sit on their own for large stretches to read and think and scribble and shape and create. But no one makes anything without others.

Brian Eno, one of the originators of **HardArt** (along with the amazing Clare Farrell and hepcat Jamie Kelsey, who gave this novel its name), is fond of talking about 'scenius' instead of 'genius'. It is the collective, collaborative scenes of people who like and often love one another (which doesn't mean they don't fight!) who create the big ideas that have a chance to reimagine the world. The music industry (where Brian mostly works) or art industry or publishing industry are, in the end, creations and mechanisms of capitalism, and operate as such. And capitalism, the economic system of (now neoliberal) 'rational' individualism, operates at maximum capitalist capacity when it privileges a very few at the expense of the majority. I mean, just look at the distribution of wealth under capital, as the international super-rich elite hoard what was once our common wealth. The myth of the 'author' in that sense is just another capitalist construction to make a handful of people lots of money.

So even if there's no point in putting another novel out into the world, not really, not in terms of an adequate or proportionate use of anyone's time in this crisis; even if we know that making art is a beautiful way of living, and that it's better than war; if we *are* going to put a novel out into the world, then it can't be done in the old capitalist model. (Not to criticise those small or independent publishers and writers who just want to make beautiful things and give others the chance to read those beautiful things, and who adopt the model because it's the only one most of us think we have.)

To put it another way: was my novel *Daddio!* **hard enough** to be a piece of **HardArt**? Not on its own. Not solely 'authored' by me.

So, here I was, lucky to be invited to the first gathering of **HardArt** (to take notes!) in November 2022; lucky to be one of the first pair to sit down and do a 'blind contour drawing' with the film-maker Leon Oldstrong, an exercise in documentation coordinated by Mr Ian Bruce, artist and singer *extraordinaire*, whose work has led to the *Drawn Without Looking* book of 100 portraits released by **HardArt** last year on Metalabel (see following pages). Here I also was, documenting the ideas and outcomes of the first **HardArt** session, where attendees considered what kind of art or institutions were needed right now, if we were to "live in the time we're in". And one of those ideas, which came collaboratively from Leon Oldstrong and the table he was on, was this idea of the ALARM CLOCK as an immersive piece of art to help people not only know but feel and understand in their body the climate crisis we are facing. And here I *also* was, in the midst of writing a new novel, a story where the fictional author was taking his fictional father to a fictional funeral, when, in real life, my father died just a few days after that first **HardArt** gathering.

And so at some point, amidst the funeral planning and family dysfunction that accompany death, I picked up the idea of the alarm clock as a piece of content, and put it in the novel (thank you Leon); and then I came to realise that I could also pick up (the word

The Alarm Clock poster from the first HardArt session, November 2022

Brian likes is 'harvest') not only the ideas *in* **HardArt** but also the idea *of* **HardArt**, as a collaborative scenius powered by love, and turn the novel into a *form* worthy of the collective, **hard enough** to challenge all those capitalist forms and fears that art might not be worth making. It *is* worth it. If this novel is a work of collaborative labour, then it is a model for the work we will have to do together now and into the future, for the world that is coming to us, whether we want it to or not.

Which is a long way of saying thank you to all those in **HardArt**, and those beyond, who have made this novel with me, and for confronting the present to challenge us to live in the times we're in. Especially Brian Eno, Clare Farrell and Jamie Kelsey for the imagination and bravery to make the scenius happen, and dearly to Charlie Waterhouse, Alanna Byrne, Nuala Lam, John Fass, Jo Rendle, Clare Patey, Liz Slade, Paul Ewan and the rest of the **HardArt** crew for the work of making it, in London and Manchester and globally. To Roc Sandford, Clive Russell, Sophie Cowen and Daze Aghaji at Absurd Intelligence for the fun, love, camaraderie and hard work. To everyone in the **HardArt** room, especially Paul (again), Jamie (again) and Bette Adriaanse for being early readers of the novel, and great collaborators. For Jeremy Deller for the cover design and Brian Eno for the musical accompaniment, to Jay Griffiths for the Foreword and loving kindness. For Ian Bruce for the portraits, Leon Oldstrong and the table for the alarm clock concept. To Yancey Strickler for the innovation of collaborative production that gets us to somewhere new. To Caro (*and* Mont, Lucy Nell, CLV!) my love.

Perhaps a novel can be an alarm clock, in the sense that it is imagined in this novel. An immersive artpiece that transports you into a space of embodied experience, of imagining a future and what it feels like to be in that future, something we need to be woken up to; what Nick Royle (after David Bowie) calls a "sun machine"; and why, above all, love (and breathing!) remains in the end all that matters.

Always remember, if you can:

Humanity is love, and love is sometimes (sometimes!) hard work.

LEON OLDSTRONG

DRAWN WITHOUT LOOKING BY

coloured in by

ALEX

DRAWN WITHOUT LOOKING BY

Leon Oldstrong

coloured in by